MW01248752

THE

DARK

ELF

TRAVIS STINNETT

Travis Stinnett
Visit my website @ www.thesilentsoldiers.com

First Paperback Edition May 2014 by Travis Stinnett.

Stinnett, Travis, 1978-
The Silent Soldiers: The Dark Elf / by Travis Stinnett.__1st ed.

Summary: Luke and his team continue to master their powers and skills. After receiving an unknown, life changing inheritance, he decides to expand the size of the Silent Soldiers force.

Their newest enemy, the Dark Elf, promises to be their greatest challenge so far. His powers are so much more difficult to deal with than anything they have ever encountered. His evil deeds are worse than they imagined to be possible.

Follow the Silent Soldiers as they discover and do battle with new enemies, increase the size of their evil fighting force, and deal with all the changes in their lives.

ISBN 978-1495216404
[1. Vampires—Fiction. 2. Young Adult—Fiction. 3. Supernatural—Fiction.]
I. Title. II. Series: Stinnett, Travis. The Silent Soldiers: The Dark Elf ; bk. 3.

ISBN-10: 1499755317
ISBN-13: 978-149955312

For my Dad. Thank you for helping me get this book together with proofreading and editing. Love you Dad!

Acknowledgments

I would like to thank my wife Crystal for continuing to encourage me through this entire writing and publishing process. This is book 3 and there are several more on the way. Thank you for supporting me. I want to thank my Dad, Billy Stinnett for the hours of proofreading and editing he has put into all three books so far in The Silent Soldiers series. I also would like to thank Cliff Pennington with Pennington Graphics Solutions for all the amazing graphics work especially the spectacular book covers for the entire novel series. I also want to thank my children as they offer inspiration and ideas that spark creative ideas to include in my writing. And thank you to all my fans that have started following The Silent Soldiers series.

Don't miss Book Four in

THE SILENT SOLDIERS SERIES:

The Supernatural Council

1

Matt and I were having a guy's day out. At least that's what we called it. The girls were having their own day out. It was only two weeks until the homecoming dance at school so the girls decided to go out shopping for dresses. We were given strict orders to do some shopping of our own. We were supposed to get fitted for our tuxes and order corsages for our dates. Matt and I finished shopping as quickly as possible. Neither of us were the shopping type if you know what I mean. We were definitely glad we weren't shopping with the girls.

Finishing early left us with nothing to do. We decided to catch a Twisters game in Little Rock. I have never been interested in football before this school year. I spent most of my free time perfecting my martial arts skills as a child instead of school sports. It had definitely come in handy over the past couple years to say the least. Normally we would only attend classes at the mansion. The four of us decided we rather go to public school than be cooped up at home all the time.

I tried out and made the football team at school. I took the position of starting quarterback for the Varsity team. Matt of course didn't want to be left out so he secured the position of wide receiver. Sure, it wasn't really fair to beat out the humans with all of our super powers. But, we were doing our best to be normal, and were having the best time of our lives. We did our best not to show off for fear of being exposed to the humans, but our team was of course undefeated.

The homecoming game, we learned, was probably the most important game to win the whole year. Matt and I could hardly wait. After we won the game we would be taking our beautiful dates to the homecoming dance.

So, here we were at the football stadium watching the Arkansas Twisters face off against the Shreveport Battlewings for a little Indoor Football League action. I sat there thinking that Matt and I could stand in for anyone of the players and dominate the game with our super powers. I only hoped that our lives could remain normal enough to have the chance someday.

Our decision to stay in public school had come with its own consequences. Not only did we have to keep up with our school work, we also had to keep up our studies at the mansion. We liked one more year before we completed our supernatural studies.

Since our last mission against the green eyed vamps, and the evil trolls, things had been fairly quiet in the supernatural community. We always had our guard up for whatever Nhados sent our way, but other than that all seemed well.

Everything, that was except for one little detail. The only female that was turned into a green eyed vamp, had cornered me on my way to the locker room the night of our first football game. Jordan told me she remembered everything from the battle in the gym the night before. Rachel had supposedly wiped the memories of all the students we had saved, but somehow her spell didn't affect Jordan. Then, to my surprise, she disappeared right before my eyes. I have been keeping a close watch out for her. I haven't seen any sign of her since that night. I haven't told anyone about my strange encounter with Jordan. I am waiting until I know more about what is going on before I alarm my friends.

Suddenly my phone went off in my pocket. I pulled it out to check the message thinking it was probably Ava letting me know they are done shopping.

"I need to talk to you," said the message from a number I didn't recognize.

"Who is this?" I replied.

"It's Jordan. I really need to talk to you, Luke. It is very important," she said.

"When? Where?" I asked confused. I had no clue what she could possibly need to talk to me about. And on top of that, how in the heck did she have my cell phone number?

"Now! Meet me outside the arena as soon as you can get away from Matt."

Now I was down right freaked out a little. How did she know where I was? Was she following me? I scanned the crowds, as fast as I could, trying to pick her out in the thousands of people that filled the arena. Even with my vampire senses I couldn't find her anywhere.

"Matt, I'll meet you at the car as soon as the game is over. I'm going to run to the bathroom before all of these people start leaving," I lied.

"Ok man. Do you want me to come with you?"

"No!" I reply a little louder than necessary. I really don't know why I was trying to hide this from Matt. If anything I could probably use all the backup I could get if something went wrong.

"Is everything ok?" Matt asked, confused by my snappy response.

"Everything is great. I'll see you when you get down there," I told him before I turned and headed for the parking lot. I didn't know where I was supposed to meet Jordan. The stadium was huge and I noticed several exits as I made my way to the front entrance. I sent her a quick text message as I went out the exit.

I walked down the steps and out of the arena as quickly as I could. People were already starting to leave so it was getting sort of crowded already. As soon as I made it out the doors I spotted Jordan sitting on the concrete wall around the flagpoles outside the front entrance. She smiled at me like every other time I had seen her. I marched over to where she sat and grabbed her by the arm. I started toward my car hoping she didn't put up a struggle. I definitely didn't want a bunch of humans overhearing whatever it was she had to tell me.

"What is the big emergency, Jordan?" I asked as soon as we made it out of hearing distance.

"What's the big hurry, Luke? Why are you dragging me like we are running from something?"

"Well, first of all I want to know if you have been following me," I told her. "How exactly did you know where to find me?"

She was making me a little irritated with her easy going attitude.

"Well, that is what my power is. I can blink to anywhere just by thinking about something. I thought about you, Luke, so here I am," Jordan said with a huge smile.

"Blink? What exactly does that mean?" I asked.

"It's sort of like teleporting I guess. The only difference is I can stay invisible whenever I get to my location."

"So, you can just jump anywhere and spy on people because you're invisible?" I asked.

I had been teleported on several occasions and there was always a flash of bright light or a puff of smoke wherever I materialized.

"That's right," she replied with the same happy smile on her face.

She failed to answer about the smoke or light part but I decided to let it go for now. I needed to remember to let her know it was not ok to sneak around and spy on people.

"What was so important that you thought you had to drag me out of the game to tell me?" I asked.

"It's not really anything I wanted to tell you. It is more like something I wanted to ask you. I need a favor, Luke."

"And what exactly would that be?" I asked.

I was starting to push past the point of irritation and go straight to anger.

"Well, I wanted to ask you to turn me," she said as she continued to smile.

I was really ready to just smack her at this point. Maybe send her flying over the arena. That surely would have been a sight for the huge crowd. But, her question caught me off guard completely.

"What do you mean turn you?"

"I mean will you turn me into one of you?" She asked.

"And what exactly do you think I am?"

"A vampire, of course. I want to be changed back into a vampire. I didn't want to be changed back to this," she said as the motioned toward herself with one hand.

The happy smile remained fixed to her face as though she couldn't stop smiling even if she wanted to.

"I don't even know how to do that. I'm not positive that I could, even if I wanted to. What exactly are you anyway?"

"I'm nothing! I'm just a stupid human with a stupid power that is absolutely worthless to me!" She shouted.

"You really need to keep your voice down. You know it is against supernatural law to reveal our true selves to humans. Tell me why you would want to be turned into a vampire in the first place."

"I want to have super powers again. I know I was under an evil spell before, but I wouldn't be under any spell if you turned me. I want to be powerful and be able to help and protect people like you and the Silent Soldiers," said Jordan.

"Whoa, how do you know about the soldiers?" I ask.

I suddenly suspected she knew a lot more than she was telling me. Probably more than she should ever know.

"I knew you wouldn't help me. I know all about you and the rest of the soldiers. I grew up hearing about the prophecies your grandmother told. I will find a way to get what I want. We elves ALWAYS find a way to get the things that we desire," Jordan said as tears began to roll down her cheeks.

"You're an elf? But, you are so much bigger than the elves I have met," I said confused about what Jordan really was.

"I'm only part elf. My mother was an elf and my father was a human. So, that makes me a half breed just like you, Luke. I'm guessing there are lots of things you still have to learn. Elves come in different sizes you know. Not all of them are the short little creatures with the pointy ears," said Jordan.

"You said was. Are your parents gone?" I asked her.

It probably wasn't the most caring question I could have asked, but I needed to figure out what was going on. I felt the need to find out more about Jordan and where she came from.

"My mother met my father in the forest where her people came from. They had a very short relationship and sometime while they were together they created me. My father never even knew I existed. As soon as my mother found out she was pregnant she ran away and never spoke to my father again. When I was old enough to take care of myself I decided to hide amongst the humans," Jordan explained.

"You realize vampire venom is deadly to an elf, right?" I asked her.

"It is only deadly to a pure blood elf."

I suddenly remembered she had been bitten by one of the green eyed vamps.

"I don't want to be a half breed anymore. I want to have super powers again," Jordan said pleading her case.

"What part of never going into the sunlight or drinking blood for all eternity sounds fun to you? I don't see that as a life somebody would choose for themselves."

I was doing my best to talk her out of whatever twisted plan she had her mind set on. I could tell she already had her mind made up, but I had to at least try to save her life. I couldn't believe she would choose a life of secrecy over continuing as a human.

"Stop playing games with me, Luke!" Jordan shrieked. I looked around and noticed several people looking at us. "This is what I want, and nothing is going to stop me," she said lowering her voice again. "Either you will help me or you want."

"Jordan, I wish you would think this through. And, I don't even know how to turn anybody. I haven't even known what I am myself for very long. I don't know that I can help you," I said trying to make her understand. I had no intention of turning her, but even if I did I wouldn't begin to know how. I tried to be as compassionate as I possibly could. I could tell she was on the verge of having a break down.

"Fine! I really wanted you to be the one to do this. If you want help me I will find somebody that will!" Jordan said raising her voice again.

I reached out to touch her arm to try and calm her down. Just before my hand made contact Jordan vanished once again right before my eyes.

I looked around nervously to see if anyone witnessed her sudden disappearance. Nobody was staring with their mouths hanging open so I guessed we were safe. I would have to remind her about the whole secrecy in front of humans law she seemed to have no regard for. The last thing I needed was to get in trouble with the council.

Suddenly Matt walked up with a huge smile on his face. He didn't notice the seriousness on mine. I smiled back at him so he didn't start to ask questions. I didn't know exactly how to handle the situation with Jordan yet. Until I figured that out I was going to continue to keep it to myself. I wondered if I would ever see Jordan again before she found some random vamp that agreed to turn her.

"We won, man! We scored another touchdown with fifteen seconds left on the clock. That was awesome!" Matt cheered.

Some of the other fans exiting the arena began cheering along with him. I definitely was not in the cheering mood.

"That's great." I told him. "I wonder if the girls are done with their shopping adventure."

"Let's find out. I'm starving!" Matt said as he pulled his phone out of his pocket and hit Jenna's speed dial number.

She told him they were finishing up at the mall. We decided to meet them there for dinner. After dinner, Ava and I were alone for the first time all day for the ride home.

"What's wrong, Luke?" Ava asked as she put her hand gently on mine.

I was doing my best to hide my encounter with Jordan and the fact that it was still bothering me. I guess I wasn't doing as good a job as I thought. I smiled at Ava and squeezed her hand gently.

"Nothing is wrong," I lie, "Why do you ask?"

"You seem like something is bothering you. I was just worried about you," Ava said.

I noticed the concern in her voice. Ava always looked out for me. I don't know why I felt I should keep Jordan a secret.

"I'm fine. I couldn't be happier," I told her as we made our exit off the freeway toward Eerie.

Ava smiled and squeezed my hand back. She didn't push the issue any further, but, she never did. That's what I loved most about her. She knew I would eventually tell her everything when the time was right.

As I tried to fall asleep I couldn't help but be worried about Jordan. What if she found a vamp to turn her, and he decided to drain her blood instead. I thought about the gruesome scene as I drifted off to sleep.

I started to dream almost instantly once I finally fell asleep. A creature unlike any I had ever seen before stands in front of me. His skin is black as coal. His eyes glow yellow. His hair matches the silver color of the blades on the weapon he holds in his hand. It hangs long and straight down his back. I can't imagine what type of creature it could be. I noticed his ears were long and pointed like those of an elf, but he seemed to be way too big.

Suddenly the creature smiled with the most evil grin. His smile revealed his pointed, razor sharp, white teeth. I watched in horror as the creature pulled an arrow into the bow he held in his hand with near vampire speed and aimed it at me. Suddenly, the creature released the arrow. I watched as it raced toward me. I looked down at my stomach and noticed the arrow had gone straight through my body. I dropped to my knees as blood began to soak through my clothes.

I woke up shooting upright in my bed back at the mansion. My clothes and the bed around me were drenched in sweat. My body continued to tremble from the fear that lingered after the nightmare I had just endured.

2

When I finally settled my nerves, realizing it was only a dream, I fell back against my bed. I didn't know how long I had been asleep. My room was completely dark regardless of the time of day. There were no windows in my room. When I first moved to the mansion it bothered me not having any sunlight shine in. It didn't take long to realize I could sleep much better with it completely dark.

I glanced over at my alarm clock and realized it was nearly ten a.m. I slowly crawled out of the bed and headed to the bathroom to take a shower. I didn't bother turning on the lights. With my vampire senses I could see just as good in the dark as I could with the light on. Sometimes I didn't even realize the lights were off. On more than one occasion when I had visitors they would have to turn on the lights when they came in my room. It seemed the longer I had my powers the more comfortable I felt with the darkness.

I got dressed and headed downstairs when I was done with my shower. The amazing smells of breakfast food had already been replaced with the wonderful aromas of pepperoni and mozzarella cheese. I guessed it would be pizza for lunch as I made my way down the stairs toward the dining room. I didn't know if it was the vampire, or the shifter sense of smell that could pick up smells so keenly. It might have been a combination of the two, but I could pick up the smallest of scents from quite amazing distances. I wondered if the other shifters could smell as good as I could. I made a mental note to talk to Matt about it sometime.

My senses also picked up two very familiar scents. I knew I would find Mom and Grandma in the dining hall before I even reached the bottom of the stairs. I was surprised to find they didn't have any food in front of them. I wondered what they could be up to. Normally they sat around in the Great room if they just wanted to chat. I headed straight for the kitchen before walking over to sit with them. I was right about the kitchen cooking pizza. I knew I would be. They already had some ready so I just grabbed a plate full of slices and a soda.

"Hi, honey," Grandma said as I sat down at the table next to her.

"Good morning, baby," Mom added. Mom always called me baby. I didn't mind when we were alone, but it was quite embarrassing when my friends were around.

"Good morning. What are y'all up to?" I asked curiously. I thought it quite odd for them to be sitting here in the dining hall. It wasn't the most comfortable place to have a conversation, and, it definitely wasn't the most private.

"We were just discussing some business." Mom said as I watched her steal a glance at Grandma.

Now I knew they were trying to hide something. I guessed they thought I was too young to pick up on their little glances they gave each other. Like when they had been talking about something they didn't want me to know, or when they discussed how exactly to tell me something.

I figured they would tell me if they wanted to so I opened my soda before taking a huge bite out of one of the slices of pizza on the plate in front of me. I saw them steal another concerned glance at each other out of the corner of my eye before Grandma spoke again.

"Luke, there is something I need to tell you."

"Ok. You know you can tell me anything Grandma. I think I have seen and been through quite enough in the past couple years for pretty much nothing to surprise me," I told her.

"I had a vision yesterday, Luke. I am afraid there is a new prophecy."

"Just tell me, Grandma. I am sure I can handle it." I said trying not to let them know I was actually nervous all of a sudden.

"The new prophecy says the evil brother will soon rise against the chosen one from deep within." Grandma said.

"The evil brother I'm afraid has already rose against me. That isn't necessarily a new prophecy, right?" I asked suddenly feeling relieved about what she was telling me. "Nhados rose from deep within the underworld a couple years back I do believe," I added a little sarcastically.

"That is true, Luke. But, if the evil brother was in fact Nhados I don't know why I would just now be seeing this prophecy."

"Well, I am positive the soldiers and I can handle anything that comes our way. We have dealt with evil before and we can do it again."

"We just need to be very careful and watch out for anything new just in case. Nhados is definitely not the only being that is out there, Luke." Mom said.

I couldn't understand why Mom and Grandma were acting so strange about this prophecy. We already know that I am destined to fight evil. We also know that Nhados is out there and continues to send his evil minions against us. What made this different than any other day?

I had finished eating by the time we were done talking about the prophecy. Mom asked if I had time to go with her down to headquarters. I wondered what she needed me for. The butterflies returned as I became nervous again on our way to the elevator.

I followed her off the elevator and noticed she was heading straight for the security booth where Dante was smiling back at us. He stood as we approached and gave Mom a quick kiss on the lips. Mom and Dante had started dating during the two years we thought my father was dead. After he was killed during the battle in England they told me about their relationship. I was relieved to find out Mom was moving on and was finally happy. I liked Dante a lot and knew he would take good care of my mother.

"Jenna is on her way," I heard Dante whisper to Mom. What exactly were they up to? Why did they want Jenna and me to come down here? I couldn't seem to put the pieces of the puzzle together as I tried to anticipate what they needed to tell us. Just then the elevator doors opened and Jenna walked over to us smiling as she always did.

"What's up Dad?" Jenna asked.

"Well, you two know that Dante and I have been seeing each other for quite some time now." Mom said. "We have a bit of good news to share with you."

"Good news?" I asked nervously. I still couldn't imagine what they were talking about. I looked over and noticed that Jenna was smiling excitedly.

"Dante has asked me to marry him," Mom said.

"That's great news!" shouted Jenna.

"Congratulations." I said trying to show as much enthusiasm as Jenna. I suddenly didn't know how I felt about this relationship. I was happy that Mom had someone to love her knowing that my father never had, but I was nervous about the thought of having a new Dad. I was even more nervous about Jenna becoming my sister. I thought it was kind of strange that when they got married my new sister would be dating my cousin. Matt was the closest thing to a sibling I ever had. Now, I was going to have a sister.

I found myself quite uncomfortable as the four of us laughed and hugged each other with the good news about the coming wedding. I was saved when Grandpa's voice came over the phones speaker.

"Dante, can you please send Luke and Sandra to the great room?"

"Right away, Mr. Carrington," replied Dante. Mom and I exchanged curious glances. What now? I thought to myself.

Mom gave Dante another kiss and a big hug before we headed to the elevator to see what Grandpa wanted. We made our way to the great room in silence. I figured Mom was just as nervous as I was about what he needed us for. We walked through the double doors and stopped dead in our tracks. Two large men in suits and ties stood next to Grandpa holding brief cases. We continued into the room and I closed the door behind me.

"Please have a seat Mr. and Mrs. Stallings," one of the men said as we made our way over to the huge table on one side of the room. "We are here on behalf of Alexander and Terry Stallings," the other man said as we took a seat across from them.

"What is this about?" Mom asked nervously. I could sense the fear in her voice.

"Your father-in-law and your husband left a will with our firm," said the first man. I suddenly realized these two men must be attorneys.

"A will?" I asked confused. I didn't know supernatural creatures did that sort of business with humans. I knew these two men were humans from their smell. I have never had the urge to drink from a human, but I can definitely relate to how other vampires must feel. I looked nervously at Grandpa.

"It's alright Luke. These men are attorneys with the supernatural council. They know all about our world," Grandpa told me.

"But they are humans," I said. I was completely shocked to find out that humans knew about the supernatural world I was destined to protect.

"The council employs a number of humans to carry out our business with the human world, Luke." I was surprised that I was hearing about it for the first time. Grandpa walked over and put his hand on my shoulder before taking a seat next to me.

"I am David Jackson and this is my partner Michael Simms. We are here to inform you, Mrs. Stallings," Mr. Jackson started.

"Please call me Sandra," Mom said as she cut the attorney off mid sentence. I no longer go by the Stallings name after the recent events that have taken place," Mom said quite coldly. I definitely couldn't blame her about that.

"Ok, Sandra, I am afraid your deceased husband and his father left everything they own to your son, Lucas Stallings," said Mr. Jackson.

I heard Mom gasp suddenly upon hearing this bit of information. I felt Grandpa's hand return to my shoulder.

"Everything?" Mom asked in a shaky voice. It almost sounded as though she were on the verge of crying.

"How could Alexander leave me everything when he didn't even know I was still alive?" I asked.

"Luke, your father knew you were alive," said Grandpa quietly. He spoke so softly that I wondered if anybody but me could have heard him.

"That is correct, Sandra. About a year ago Alexander and Terry came to our firm and had us draw up a new will for the both of them. Terry has left Lucas an estate that includes this amount," Mr. Simms said as he slid a piece of paper in front of my mother and me. I looked down at the paper and immediately noticed an amount typed on the paper. My father had left me three million dollars. I was absolutely speechless.

"Alexander's estate is much more involved than his son's. On top of a very large sum of money, Alexander owned a large number of real estate properties. He also owned a large corporation. We were not informed about what this corporation consists of," said Mr. Simms.

"Alexander also owned a private jet that will arrive at the Little Rock airport at nine a.m. in the morning to bring Lucas to England. He must come immediately to sign the paperwork and make his preparations to take over his family's business," said Mr. Jackson.

"I can't just run off to England. I have school in the morning," I told the men. I know school was probably the least of my worries at that point, but I didn't want to lose my grip on what humanity I had left. Nobody in that room could possibly understand just how important going to school was to me.

"Luke, don't worry about school. We will take care of everything. You must take care of business first," whispered Grandpa.

"We will be here at eight a.m. in the morning to accompany you to the airport. Your flight leaves at nine sharp for England, Lucas," Mr. Jackson told me.

I didn't know what to say. In a matter of minutes I had changed from a kid finding out his Mom was getting remarried, to a billionaire business tycoon. I was absolutely speechless.

3

The attorneys packed up their things and Grandpa escorted them to the front door. I continued to stay where I was completely shocked by what I had just found out. I could hear Mom saying my name right beside me but I couldn't seem to snap out of the trance I was in. I finally came to when Mom started to shake me and ask if I was alright.

"I'm ok, Mom. I lied. I didn't know that I would be ok for quite some time.

"Luke, tell me what you're thinking," she said.

"I don't really know what to think. I never even met him, Mom."

"Met who, baby? What are you talking about?"

"I never met my grandfather, Alexander. Why would he leave me everything?"

"Well, I do have a theory about that, Luke. From what we learned about your father trying to force you to his side I think it's safe to say they hoped you would use this money and power to carry out their evil bidding," Mom explained.

"But I refuse to be involved in any evil business, Mom. You know that."

"I know, honey. Just because you have inherited all of this doesn't mean you have to use it for evil. Right?"

"That's right," I said as I began to understand what she was meaning. I was in complete control of the situation. I could do whatever I wanted to do with their money because it was all mine now. I didn't have to use it for evil. I could use it to help people. I could use it to do the work the Silent Soldiers were created for. Money had never been an issue with Grandpa being so wealthy, but I had an idea. I suddenly began to get excited about the journey that would begin in the morning.

"I'm going to pack, Mom. You are going with me aren't you?" I asked.

"I will go if you want me to, baby."

"Well, of course I want you to, Mom. Why wouldn't I?" I said with a smile. Mom smiled back as she pulled me into a hug.

"I love you, Luke. I am so very proud of the man you are turning into."

"Mom, I want Ava to go with us. I would rather take the whole team, but if something goes wrong over there I may need Ava for backup."

I really just wanted Ava close to me. It would be nice having her there just in case, but that isn't the main reason I wanted her to go.

"We will have to ask Rachel if she will allow her to go. I don't mind if her mother says it's ok."

"I'll go talk to her. You should get packed too, Mom." I said as I headed out the doors into the foyer.

I bolted up the stairs in vampire speed headed for Ava's room. I was knocking on her door in a fraction of a second.

Rachel answered the door and began to smile when she realized it was me.

"Hey, Luke. How are you?" Rachel asked.

"I'm fine. Is Ava around?"

"Sure. I'll go get her for you."

"Actually Mrs. Hadison I really need to speak to the both of you if you have a minute."

"Of course. Come on in. Is something wrong?"

"Nothing is wrong. I just found out some very important news that I need to tell you about."

Ava came in from the bathroom and walked over to take a seat next to me.

"What's up, Luke?" Ava asked as she took a seat next to me on the couch. I started in with the events of the day. I took the time to tell them about Grandma's new prophecy and about Mom and Dante getting married. Then I started in on the news about my inheritance. I think they were in as much shock as I was when I heard it for the first time.

"So that brings me to what I needed to tell you, or ask you," I told them as they continued to stare at me in shock, "I wanted to ask you if Ava could go with Mom and me to England," I told Rachel. I waited for a response before I pleaded my case. I saw the excitement flash into Avas' eyes.

"Well, Luke, that is definitely a big request. How long will you be gone?" Rachel asked.

"I don't know for sure exactly. I have to go and sign a bunch of paperwork, and I have to make sure my grandfather's business is in order. Grandpa says we will figure something out about school so we don't get behind. I told Mom I would rather take the whole team with me, but I don't think it would be good for us all to be absent at the same time. They might start to get suspicious since we all missed together not very long ago.

"And your mother is going with you, right?"

"Yes ma'am. Mom is going with us for sure. We leave in the morning at nine on my…"

"On your what?" Ava asked curiously. I suddenly realized she was hanging on my every word. I knew she was just as excited as I was about this trip.

"On my jet." I told them. That felt like the strangest thing I had ever said. I couldn't grasp the concept of suddenly being a billionaire with my own private jet.

"You have to promise me you will take care of my baby," Rachel said.

"You know I will," I said smiling at Ava. I watched her blush and realized she was just as embarrassed as I was with our moms calling us baby.

"I know you will, Luke. I trust you," Rachel told me.

"Let's go to your room, Luke," Ava said.

We stood and walked the short distance down the hall to my room. I asked Ava to help me decide which clothes to take with me. We stood in my closet looking through our options.

"All you have is jeans and t-shirts, Luke."

"That is all I own. I have never had any reason to get anything any nicer to wear."

"Looks like we have some shopping to do," she said smiling over at me. In a flash I used my vampire speed to rush over to Ava and take her in my arms. I heard her gasp as I put my lips gently to hers.

"What was that for?" She asked as she looked up into my smiling face.

"I'm lucky to have you. And I am so happy your mom is letting you come with me."

I watched as her eyes filled with tears and threatened to spill over. I knew in my heart they were tears of joy. She laid her face into my chest hugging me close so I couldn't see her crying. I knew she was from the smell of the tears as they began to stream down her face.

"I love you, Luke."

"I love you too, Ava." Ava stopped by to let her Mom know we were going to the mall. I sent Mom a quick message from my phone to let her know as well. I told Ava I would meet her at headquarters. I need to talk to Grandpa and let him know I needed to use the credit card. I promised him I would be paying the bill myself from now on. He said that would be fine. Next, I headed down to meet Ava.

I'm not much of a shopper, but I was actually excited about getting to the mall. I think I was more excited about the trip the next day than anything else. I could tell Ava was excited as well. She couldn't seem to be still in her seat and she was rambling on and on about the things I would need.

We went to several different stores before Ava finished shopping for me. I came out with three suits complete with matching shoes, ties, and belts. She also picked out a couple casual pant and shirt sets. I was definitely glad to have her along to help me. I hate shopping. Next it was her turn to shop. I told her to pick out some formal outfits as well. She told me she had some things she could take but I wanted her to have new things for the trip just like me. She was ecstatic as she rushed from store to store trying to pick out the perfect outfits.

It was almost dark by the time we made it back to the mansion. Matt and Jenna were at headquarters when we made it back and parked the car. Luckily they were there and could help us carry everything up to our rooms. I had splurged a little and bought us both a set of luggage. I didn't know if Ava had any, but I knew I didn't.

"Wow y'all went on a shopping spree didn't you?" Matt asked. I forgot that Matt and Jenna didn't know that we were leaving in the morning. I tried to bring them up to speed about everything that happened as we made our way upstairs. I got the same shocked reaction from both of them.

"We leave in the morning for England," I told them as I started to get my stuff together and started packing.

"Who is we?" asked Jenna.

"Mom, me, and Ava are going. I really wanted all of us to go, but I don't think it is wise for everybody to miss school at the same time."

"So, you're actually a billionaire?" Matt asked.

"I guess so," I told him.

"So, you're going to bring your little sis something amazing back from England, Right?" Jenna asked with a huge grin on her face. I was definitely caught off guard with that. I never had a sister before. It seemed as though Jenna was definitely alright with the wedding and having me as a brother.

"Of course!" I said smiling back at her.

"Sis?" Ava asked confused.

I realized I had forgotten to tell Ava about Mom and Dante. I guessed it had slipped my mind with all the other news about my inheritance. I quickly brought Ava up to speed.

"How are you guys getting there? Grandpa's plane is away on business isn't it?" Matt asked.

"We are taking Luke's jet!" Ava exclaimed!

"What? You have a jet too?" Matt asked excitedly.

"Apparently I have a lot of things now," I told him shyly. I had always heard that money changes people. I believed it was the other way around. I believed that money changes the people around you. I definitely didn't want my friends and family to be different now that I had money.

Matt and Jenna excused themselves and headed out of the room. I figured they were heading to Matt's to make out. It had definitely become a steady habit of theirs lately I thought to myself. The more I thought about it the more I wouldn't have minded a little make out action myself. I finished packing the rest of my stuff and put it next to the door. I looked over and saw Ava smiling back at me. I used my vampire speed and before she could even blink I was on my knees in front of her with my lips pressed gently to hers. I again heard her gasp at my sudden appearance so close to her. I pulled back slightly and whispered to her,

"Did I scare you?"

"Yeah a little bit, but I don't mind."

"Do you want me to stop?" I hoped she didn't want me to stop. It was an amazing feeling taking a girls' breath away by getting close to her.

"You better not!" Ava exclaimed as she pulled me back to kiss her again. It was getting kind of late, but I didn't want to stop kissing Ava. I never wanted to stop kissing or being with her. "You know we have an early start in the morning," Ava told me.

"Yes. I know we do, but I can't seem to get enough of this," I said as I pressed my lips to hers again. I felt Ava giggling as she tried to pull back away from me. She finally gave up after a few seconds. She knew she could never break my embrace if I didn't want her to. A few seconds later I pulled back and stood up slowly. I pulled her up out of the chair by her hands and straight into my arms. I hugged her close for several seconds before I let her go. I took her by the hand and walked her to her room.

"I love you," Ava said.

"I love you too," I replied.

She kissed me before quickly turning and going into her room. I stood there staring at her door for several seconds before I headed back to my own room.

With everything I had been through that day I fell asleep thinking only of the girl I was madly in love with. My decision had been made. Ava was definitely the girl of my dreams. She was the girl I wanted to spend the rest of my life with.

As I drifted off to sleep, the dream started the same as it had the night before. I could feel the fear growing stronger the minute I laid eyes on the silver haired creature before me. The same glowing yellow eyes, the same coal black skin. The silver from the creatures' weapon glistened in the sunlight. Sunlight I thought to myself. This definitely had to be something other than a vampire. But what could it be?

I tried to run but my body wouldn't move even though I was begging it to with all my might. I tried to reach for my sword but my arm wouldn't move either. It was as if I was completely paralyzed.

"Who are you?" I asked the creature. At least my voice seemed to work. The creature only smiled back at me revealing the sharp pointed teeth. "What do you want?" I asked not knowing if the creature even knew how to speak English. I watched as the creatures smile faded and was slowly replaced with a snarl. He crouched down ready to jump as he began to hiss. I noticed he was no longer staring at me. Instead, his attention seemed to be focused on something beside me. I still could not move my body enough to even turn my head to see what it was he was looking at.

All of a sudden the creature shot toward me at super human speed. I had never heard of anything that moves as fast as a vampire but this thing was definitely fast. The creature slashed out toward my head. I couldn't move at all. The only thing I could do was scream.

The dream suddenly flashed to a different scene. What I was looking at instantly caused me to break out in heavy sobs. I could feel myself shaking uncontrollably. I stood above a gruesome site of a body lying on the ground. Blood poured onto the pavement from the nearly decapitated head and neck. The face from the body was turned toward me so I could clearly see who the person was. The creature was no longer anywhere to be found, but before he left he managed to end my life.

I immediately woke up from the dream. My body shook from not only fear, but also from the uncontrollable sobs that rocked my body as I lay there clutching my pillow like a child cuddling a teddy bear. The scariest thing I could ever, and would ever face anytime in my entire life would have to be my own death. What was I going to do?

4

I didn't know what time it was, but there was no way on earth I could ever go back to sleep after that horrific dream. I rolled over in the bed to look at the alarm clock after I calmed myself enough for my body to obey my commands again. It was five a.m. I grabbed my cell phone from the bedside table. I quickly typed in a message and hit send. Less than five minutes later there was a brisk knock at the door. I slowly made my way over to answer it.

I tried to wipe away the tears from my face and eyes before opening the door. I must have looked pretty bad because Dakota instantly went from smiling to a look of great concern as he stared at me from the open doorway.

"Luke, what's wrong man?" He asked as he reached over and placed his hand on my shoulder.

"Come in and let's talk," was all I managed to tell him. I turned and walked toward the sitting area in my room leaving Dakota to close the door himself before joining me. Dakota sat in the chair across from me with his elbows on his knees. He patiently awaited my explanation of what had me so upset and calling him at this time of the morning. I knew he was ready to go to bed for the day, but I had to talk to him.

"Dakota I need your help."

"Of course, Luke. You know I owe you my life. I would do anything for you."

"I don't know if you have heard, but Ava and I are headed to England in a few hours."

"Mike told me about that. He said you had to go over to take care of some kind of inheritance business."

I didn't try to explain all the details to him. He seemed to already know enough about what was going on.

"Yes. I need you to go with us." I told him. I began to describe both of the dreams I had about the horrific silver haired creature before I allowed him to respond to my request. When I got to the part about seeing my body dead on the ground in front of me I almost started crying again. Dakotas' eyes grew large from the shock of what I was telling him.

"Luke! You need to tell Mr. Carrington about this immediately. He must set up some type of protection for you," he said ecstatically.

"No!" I shouted. I do not want to worry my friends or family about something that might not even come true. The visions I have never really end up occurring exactly the way I see them. This could even be some kind of mind trick by Nhados. We don't know anything for sure yet. That is why I want you to come with me." I explained.

Suddenly Dakota jumped out of his chair and rushed to my side at super speed. I turned quickly to see what he was doing. I was shocked to see him holding a terrified Cameron by the neck. His feet kicked wildly in the air from his suspended position. "Dakota! No!" I shouted. "Let Cam go!" I told him.

Cam is an elf. He is very short at only three feet tall. He is the son of Jack. Jack protected me from an attack by Nhados a few years back. The first time I met Cam was when he came to request my help in saving Jack's life from a vampire bite. Ava and I saved Jack resulting in Cam pledging his life to protect me. I watched as Dakota now held the little elf in the air with one hand.

"Put him down Dakota," I repeated. He slowly lowered Cam to the floor and walked backward toward the chair he had been sitting in. He never took his eyes off the tiny elf as he sat back down.

"Cam, what are you doing here?" I asked.

"I sensed you were in trouble, Luke. I came as quickly as I could," Cam explained.

"I only had a nightmare, buddy. I'll be fine," I told him. I thought to myself it was definitely a good thing I wasn't in any real danger. I would have been dead for sure as long as it took him to get to me. I didn't tell Cam what I was thinking. He was a very emotional little creature. "Thanks for coming, Cam."

"Who is he?" Cam asked as he pointed a tiny little finger toward Dakota. Cam tried to look angry toward Dakota but I could tell he was more terrified than anything.

"This is Dakota. He is a member of the Silent Soldiers," I said realizing Cam had never met all of the soldiers. Ava and I were the only two that Cam knew. I made a mental note to introduce him to everybody. I felt that Cam would probably be around fairly often and I didn't want anybody to hurt him not knowing who he was.

"Are you sure you're ok?" Cam asked me.

"I'm positive Cam."

"If you ever need my help all you have to do is call my name and I will be here."

"Ok, Cam. I will. Dakota and I have some important business to discuss now," I told Cam. I didn't need for him to overhear anything I was talking about. I saw the look of disappointment on his face as he disappeared from the room.

"I will gladly go with you, Luke." Dakota said as soon as Cam was gone.

"Thank you. I will make arrangements for you to be transported with us. We leave the airport at nine."

"I must go and get my things ready before daylight. My bags will be sitting next to my coffin."

"Thanks again Dakota." Dakota gave a little bow of his head before he left the room to prepare for the trip. I stood and walked toward the bathroom. It was still very early but I knew I couldn't go back to sleep even if I tried.

I stood in the shower for over half an hour letting the warm water calm me as much as possible. I still couldn't get the dream out of my head no matter what I tried to think about. It was after six by the time I got out and got dressed in one of the more casual outfits Ava picked out for me at the mall. I could smell the slightest hint of bacon frying from the kitchen downstairs so I knew they were already preparing breakfast. I finished putting on my new shoes and belt before I headed downstairs to eat.

There were several people already in the dinning hall. A lot of the shifters that lived at the mansion had jobs in the city. I never really had time to get to know everybody, but they all knew me for sure. I had no idea about the names of the shifters that told me "hello" and "good morning Luke" on my way to the kitchen. I took a tray filled with eggs, bacon, sausage, biscuits smothered in gravy, and a huge stack of pancakes back out into the dinning hall to eat. I met Grandpa as I headed to my usual spot at one of the tables.

"Well, good morning Luke. You are definitely looking very professional in your new attire. Are you ready for your big trip?"

"Definitely. I'm looking forward to it, actually."

"You have a lot to look forward too. I want you to know you can call me for anything, Luke. If you need any help or advice, call me anytime day or night," Grandpa told me.

"Thanks Grandpa. I will definitely call you."

Grandpa headed off to the kitchen after patting me on the back. I sat down and started eating. I was sitting with my back toward the doorway when suddenly a set of arms wrapped around my waist and hugged me. I tried to act surprised by Ava's coming up behind me. I didn't tell her that I picked up her amazing scent before she even made it down the stairs.

"Good morning," I said as I turned my head toward hers and kissed her neck. I loved her mesmerizing smell as I held my nose against her neck taking it in. I found that everyone I came across had their own unique scent. Ava's, of course, was the most special to me. I felt certain that I could pick her out of a crowd of thousands of people by her scent alone.

"Good morning. You look absolutely stunning, my big, strong, handsome business man."

"You are quite beautiful yourself," I told her after I turned around and noticed she was wearing the outfit I had picked out for her at the mall the day before.

"Thanks. Are you as excited as I am? I couldn't hardly sleep last night I was so excited." I had slept pretty well myself until I was murdered in the horrifying nightmare I thought to myself. If I didn't want to worry Ava about my vision I probably would have called her first instead of Dakota. That reminded me I needed to make arrangements for Dakota to go with us. I pulled out my cell phone and sent Dante a quick message to see if he could take care of it. He replied back that he would make sure Dakota made it safely on the plane.

"We are taking Dakota with us," I told Ava. I tried to sound as casual as possible. I didn't want her to suspect anything might be wrong. I wanted Ava to be absolutely worry free for the trip. She mentioned after our last trip to England that she would love to visit again without all the fighting we did before. I was looking forward to taking Ava for some sight seeing adventures at some point.

"Ok. Is everything ok?" She asked curiously.

"Everything is great," I lied. I wasn't about to tell her I may need protection from a black silver haired creature that might kill me at any moment. I guess she believed me because she changed the subject.

"I made sure to pack plenty of spell orbs to take with us just in case," Ava said. I was really glad she was going to be prepared. I hoped we didn't run into any trouble, but I never knew when my visions might take place. I had already packed my sword for sure. There was no way I was going anywhere without it.

"Sounds like a great idea. I guess we should get our bags downstairs and get ready to leave before too long." Just then Mom came into the dinning hall and walked over to us.

"Good morning guys. The car will arrive soon to take us to the airport. We need to leave within the hour to make our flight on time," she told us.

"Ok, Mom. We are all packed and ready. We just need to bring our bags downstairs."

"Ok, baby. I'm going to eat some breakfast and I'll be ready to go." Mom headed off toward the kitchen while Ava and I made our way upstairs. We met Matt and Jenna coming down the hall.

"You guys getting ready to go?" Jenna asked.

"I wish we were going with you," said Matt.

"It's too bad we decided to go to public school or we could all be going for sure," I said smiling.

"Yeah well I like going to school. And I definitely love playing football," Matt said smiling back at me.

"Bring us back a souvenir," said Jenna.

"Definitely!" said Ava.

"You guys need some help with your bags?" Matt asked.

"That would be great!" I told him. We carried our bags downstairs and put them in the trunk of the car. Grandpa and the two attorneys came out the front door just as we finished loading all of our bags. He walked over and hugged Ava and then hugged me.

"Y'all be careful. Luke, if you need me for anything at all no matter how small you think it might be don't hesitate to call," said Grandpa. I wondered why he kept reinforcing the fact that I could call him. I knew even without him telling me that I could call if I needed something.

"Ok Grandpa. I will definitely keep that in mind. Do you know if Mom is ready?"

"I have someone getting her bags as we speak. She ran downstairs to speak with Dante before she leaves." Two of the younger shifters came out the front door and loaded Mom's suitcases along with ours. By the time they got the bags loaded and the trunk lid closed Mom was walking down the steps toward us.

"Are we ready?" She asked.

"I believe we are," I replied. We told Grandpa good bye and climbed into the back of the car. In no time at all we were heading down the highway toward Little Rock.

"Mr. Stallings, the appointment to sign all of the paperwork for your inheritance is not until tomorrow morning. You should have plenty of time to rest before then. Tomorrow is definitely going to be a long day," said Mr. Jackson.

We made the exit off the freeway headed for the airport. I watched out the window as the car pulled through the gate leading to the private hangars. I was familiar with this area of the airport from our recent trip on Grandpas' jet. Grandpa owned one of the hangars where his plane was stored when it wasn't being used.

Instead of making the turn toward the hangars the car went straight toward the runways. A few seconds later the car stopped and the engine was turned off. The back door opened and the driver motioned for us to get out. I was the last one out of the car and I looked at what Mom and Ava were already staring at. Sitting before us was a beautiful solid black plane. There were no markings on it to distinguish it as belonging to anybody. The steps into the cab were extended and ready for us to board. A little fat man at least a foot shorter than me was standing next to the steps of the plane. He was wearing a black suit and tie with a navy blue shirt underneath the jacket.

"You must be Mr. Stallings," said the man as we approached the plane," My name is Grady Phillips, "I was your grandfathers' pilot. I would love to be your pilot as well."

"You can call me Luke, Mr. Phillips. If Alexander was pleased with your services then I would love to have you stay on board." A smile spread across Grady's face as he reached out to shake my hand.

"And please call me Grady, Luke." After I shook his hand he motioned for us to board the plane. I noticed the driver of the limo was loading our bags from the trunk into the cargo area of the plane. I was the first one on the plane and I stopped just inside the door blocking everyone else from boarding. The inside was even more beautiful than the outside. Thick brown carpet covered the floor completely. The walls and seats were a light tan colored leather and matched perfectly the color of the carpet.

After several seconds of trying to take in the beauty of the planes interior I felt Ava nudge me in the back. I walked slowly down the isle toward the back. I turned around quickly when I realized we were forgetting something.

"We forgot Dakota!" I said excitedly.

"Dakota is already on board. If you will continue through that door you can see for yourself," Mr. Simms said motioning toward a door at the back of the plane. I turned around and went through the door. This room, I called it a room, was dimly lit by a row of tiny LED lights running down the sides of the plane There were no windows in this room. Down both sides, where seats would normally be located, were metal racks that could hold two coffins on either side like bunk beds. I knew this because Dakotas' coffin was already strapped into place on one side.

I also noticed a set of bunk beds on either side of the plane at the end of the coffin racks. Each of the bunk areas had a black curtain that could be pulled all the way across for privacy. I was mesmerized by the beauty and conveniences this plane had to offer compared to the one Grandpa owned. I turned around to head back out and nearly ran right into Ava. I didn't even realize she had followed me in.

"I'm sorry. I just about ran you over," I said smiling down at Ava as I took her into my arms.

"I didn't want to bother you while you took in this beautiful plane. It is amazing by the way," said Ava as she smiled back at me. I gave her a quick kiss before heading back to the front. I hadn't noticed before, but this plane even had a flight attendant. A lady that appeared to be about my mothers age now stood at the front of the plane smiling at us.

"There is a bathroom and a small kitchen area just inside this door," said Mr. Jackson motioning toward the door at the front of the plane, "Beyond that is the cockpit."

"The flight attendant's name is Lucy. She can hear if you speak to her, but she is unable to speak," said Mr. Simms.

Lucy smiled at us before turning to go through the door toward the kitchen. I wondered to myself what would cause her to not be able to speak.

The seats on the plane were arranged in little booths like at a restaurant. Two sets of seats faced each other with a small coffee style table on the floor between each one. Mom sat across from Ava and me in one of the booths. The two attorneys took the booth across the isle from us. Grady was in the process of closing the door of the plane as we all buckled our seat belts to prepare for departure.

"Everyone ready?" Grady asked once the door was secured.

"I believe we are," said Mr. Jackson.

Grady went in toward the cockpit closing the door behind him.

"I must warn you that this plane travels much faster than probably any other plane you have ever been on," Mr. Simms told us, "Alexander and his team of scientists designed and engineered it to get him anywhere in the world as quickly as possible. The normal flight from the U.S. to England only takes five short hours.

"Wow!" I said. I had prepared myself for a long flight, but we would touch down in England shortly after lunch.

Suddenly the plane started moving. In a matter of minutes we were jetting down the runway. Ava reached over and grabbed my hand as the plane lifted off the ground and started to climb higher into the air. A few seconds later the plane leveled out and we were on our way to England.

5

Surprisingly, even though I could feel the plane was traveling very fast, we were still able to move around the plane easily without falling. About two hours into the flight I started to pick up the scent of some type of meat cooking as well as potatoes. I knew Lucy must be preparing lunch.

"Mr. Stallings, after the plane lands, your car will take you to your penthouse in Birmingham. That is where you will be staying tonight. Our office is located on the seventeenth floor of your building," Mr. Jackson said.

"My building?" I asked, "I thought we would be staying at Alexander's castle."

"The building in Birmingham is where your grandfather conducted most of his business. He only used the castle as a sort of vacation home," Mr. Simms added. The two attorneys laughed together. They weren't really laughing at me. They laughed at what I said. I guessed I had a lot to learn about Alexander's lifestyle and the way he conducted business.

The door at the front of the plane opened and Lucy came out pushing a small metal cart. She pushed it down the isle and stopped between the two booths. She pulled the lid covering the plates revealing their contents. The most appetizing steak and fully loaded baked potato filled the plate. She continued until everyone had a plate and silverware sitting in front of them.

She pushed the cart back to the kitchen and returned with a tray full of glasses filled with ice and a pitcher with what I guessed was tea. I didn't care for tea so I asked for a coke instead. Lucy quickly went to the kitchen and returned with the can of soda. The smell coming from the food in front of me made my mouth water. We all ate in silence enjoying the wonderful meal Lucy had prepared. Lucy took away the dishes when everyone was finished with their meal.

"I think I will take a nap. I'm kind of sleepy now that my stomach is full," I told Mom and Ava.

"That sounds like a great idea. I think I will join you," Mom said.

"Me too," said Ava. We all stood and made our way to the back of the plane. I picked a bed and closed the curtain behind me. In no time I was sound asleep. I started to dream immediately.

This dream was quite a bit different from the ones before. The same silver haired creature stood before me. This time we were in a different location. Another difference I realized was this time when I tried to draw my sword I could actually move. This thing would have a much harder time trying to kill me this time, I thought. I watched as the creature jumped into the air. As it started to come down toward me I prepared for the impact. To my surprise, the creature flew over my head and landed a short distance behind me. I turned quickly to realize the creature had an arrow already in his bow. I was shocked to see who he was taking aim at. He released the arrow and it soared through the air at super speed. I jumped into action but I didn't get there in time as the arrow sliced through the persons' chest. I caught the lifeless body just in time before it crashed to the ground. Tears began to stream down my face as I lowered Ava to the ground.

I woke up and sat up quickly. I bumped my head on the bunk above me and fell back against the pillow. At least it didn't kill me this time, I thought. I was suddenly even more upset than before realizing the target may in fact be Ava instead of me. I didn't know how long I had been asleep but I decided to get up anyway. I walked back toward the front of the plane. "Mr. Jackson stopped me on my way through to the bathroom.

"It shouldn't be long before our arrival into Birmingham," he said. I nodded my head and continued on to the bathroom. I noticed the door to the cockpit was open when I came out so I stuck my head in to have a look.

"Hi, Luke. Is everything ok back there?" asked Grady.

"Everything is fine. I just saw the door open and wanted to have a look. I have never seen a cockpit before."

"Well come on in and have a seat. There is nothing like looking out of the plane from its cockpit." I climbed into the empty seat next to Grady and looked out the huge windows in front of us.

"It is beautiful!" I exclaimed. I watched as Grady pushed a button and said,

"Please prepare for arrival." Grady moved the steering device he was holding forward slightly and I could feel the plane start to descend. He slowly pulled back a lever between the two seats and the plane began to decrease in speed. I looked down in the distance and spotted the runways of the airport.

"Should I go to the back?" I asked.

"You can stay if you like. Would you like to learn how to land the plane?"

"Sure!" I said excitedly, "That would be amazing."

Grady told me to take hold of the steering device that was in front of me. He told me to hold it and get a feel of the motions he was making with his. I watched and listened as he told me each step of what he was doing as he prepared to land the plane. I was surprised to find out it seemed pretty simple as far as what he did inside the plane. I knew it definitely took precision in actually maneuvering it to make the landing at just the right place on the runway. I was happy he let me stay up there with him for the landing.

"That was awesome," I told him after the plane stopped inside a large hangar at the airport.

"Anytime, Luke. If you fly anywhere near as much as your grandfather did maybe I can teach you how to fly this thing by yourself."

"That would definitely be cool!" I exclaimed.

I got up and headed to the back. Grady continued shutting down the planes engine. Mom and Ava had returned to their seats when I made it back. When Grady was done he came back and opened the door so we could exit the plane.

We walked off the plane to find a limo, much like the one Grandpa owned, parked close to the plane. A man I assumed to be the driver was loading our luggage into the back of it. The back door was opened and we followed Mr. Jackson and Mr. Simms into the back of the limo. We heard the front door of the limo close and the window separating us from the driver lowered slowly.

"We're going straight to the office, Thomas," said Mr. Jackson.

"Yes, sir," replied Thomas with a heavy English accent.

I realized for the first time that Thomas was the first person we had encountered that actually had an English accent. Neither the attorneys nor Grady had any accent at all. I wondered where they were from. They definitely were not from England.

We rode quietly in the limo as we made our way into downtown Birmingham. I looked out the window at the enormous city around us. It took about twenty minutes before the car pulled up to the curb and stopped. I got out of the car and looked up at the building in front of us. The building was huge. I couldn't believe that I now owned it. I didn't have time to look at it much before Mr. Jackson said;

"If you follow us we will show you to your penthouse, Lucas." We followed them through the lobby area of the building. There was a large semi circle shaped counter to one side of the room with a lady sitting behind it wearing a headset.

"Stallings international. This is Wendy, How may I direct your call?" The lady behind the counter said into the headset. She said the same thing several times before we made it to a set of elevators across the room. I noticed there were several number buttons. There was also a button with the letter B and one with the letter P. I guessed the b stood for basement. I watched as Mr. Jackson stuck a key in a slot and turned it before pushing the letter P. I assumed the button stood for penthouse since that was where we were apparently going.

"This is the key to your penthouse, Mr. Stallings," Mr. Simms told me as he handed me the little gold key attached to a keychain with a large S on it. There was a second key on the ring as well.

"Please, call me Luke," I told them, "I'm too young for everybody to be calling me Mr. Stallings."

"Ok, Luke. Your penthouse is located on the top floor. As I said before our office is on the seventeenth. The basement is also a restricted area. It requires the other key on the keychain I gave you. Your grandfather's research facility is located there. Floors one thru twenty-eight are all leased to various businesses. We will go over all of that tomorrow. It is only one of the sources of your new income. The twenty-ninth floor is where your grandfather's office is located," Mr. Jackson explained. "Well, I guess it is your office now, Luke," he added.

"Ok," I said. That definitely seemed easy enough. I only had three floors I really needed to worry about. The rest were all leased to other businesses.

The elevator stopped and the doors opened to a large open area. Windows lined the entire wall in front of us I noticed as we stepped out into the room. There was a sitting area with two couches facing each other with a large coffee table in the middle. To one side was a kitchen with all the normal amenities. On the other side of the room there was a solid wall all the way down that contained four doors.

"There is a bathroom, two guest rooms, and the master suite," Mr. Jackson said as he pointed to each of the doors, "If you need anything my number is on this card. I also wrote Thomas' number on the back in case you need the car to take you anywhere. You have the rest of the afternoon free if you would like to see the sights of the city. I took the liberty of making reservations for you all at your restaurant for seven o'clock this evening."

Oh, great. I even had my own restaurant now. What didn't I own? I asked myself.

The two attorneys dismissed themselves reminding us to call if we needed anything. I pulled out my cell phone and added their phone number to my contact list. I also added the number to my limo driver. I threw the card in the trash. It was just one more thing I would have to keep up with.

Mom walked over to one of the doors and looked in. Ava took my hand and followed Mom. We walked from room to room taking in the beauty and elegance of each room. The bedroom was completely blacked out. I knew it was the only way vampires would have been able to sleep here during the day. We entered the master suite last. The room was quite simple. The floor was covered with thick white carpet from wall to wall. In the center of one wall of the room was a giant bed with all white linen and pillows. The walls were a dark brown wood with a number of different paintings hanging around the room.

There was a door leading into a bathroom which also had a large walk in closet. It was still filled with clothes I assumed belonged to Alexander. I also noticed a door on one wall. I walked over pulling Ava by the hand and opened the door. I pushed it open and definitely did not expect what I found. The door led out onto a balcony overlooking the beautiful city. There were several outdoor chairs and a small table. I pulled Ava close to me as we looked out at the city below.

"It's absolutely amazing!" Ava exclaimed.

"Am I dreaming, or is all of this actually happening?" I asked. Nobody responded as we continued to look out over the city.

We decided to call the limo driver to take us on a sight seeing tour of the city. I told him to take us to some of the most popular places. We got out to look around a few times, but other than that we just rode around and took in the sights. The city was so big that we had plenty to do and see before time for dinner. The car pulled up in front of the restaurant. We climbed out of the car before the driver even had time to make it around to open our door. We were all a little tired of riding.

I looked up at the sign on the front of the building and realized the name of it was Alexander's. I thought it was funny that a vampire owned a restaurant being that they don't eat food. I also found it off that he would name it after himself. I could tell from the outside that this was a very fancy restaurant. There was a valet service out front parking cars. All of the customers going in were dressed in suits and dresses. I was glad we hadn't decided to change into our jeans and t-shirts before we left the apartment.

"Welcome to Alexander's. What name is your reservation under?" asked the hostess behind the podium. She spoke with the familiar English accent I was starting to get used to.

"Um, try Stallings," I said not knowing what name Mr. Jackson had given them.

"Right this way, Mr. Stallings. Your room is ready. Please forgive me for not recognizing you," the lady said. I could tell she was very upset thinking she had made a huge mistake. How would she even begin to know who I was? It's not like she had ever met me before.

"It's fine ma'am. Don't worry about it," I told her. We followed the lady through the amazing restaurant and through a door into a separate room. This room contained several chairs and couches scattered around. There was a large round table in the center with a chandelier that hung down over the center. The lighting was dim but plenty bright enough for having a meal. The table had enough seating for several people. We walked over and sat down together. The hostess handed us each a menu and told us the waiter would be with us soon.

I noticed first the prices on the menu. I was quite shocked at how expensive everything seemed to be. I told Mom and Ava to order anything they wanted. I was prepared to pay the bill no matter how much it cost. I didn't really think about the fact that I owned the place.

The waiter brought in drinks for us and sat them down. We were so focused on discussing the beauty of the restaurant that I didn't even look at my glass before taking a drink. I almost sprayed the warm liquid out of my mouth realizing it wasn't water or coke I had drank. I was horrified when I looked down and realized that it was blood! How had I not smelled it? I should have known there was blood around before it even came in the room.

After I got over the shock of what I was drinking I realized the flavor inside my mouth of the blood resting on my tongue was unlike anything I had ever consumed. I closed my eyes nearly unable to control my own motions as I slowly allowed the liquid to move down my throat toward my stomach. Once the amazing taste left my mouth I suddenly felt I needed it to be returned. I unknowingly took another larger drink from the glass. If I had known what I was doing I would have never swallowed the first drink. I definitely would never have taken a second one.

I suddenly noticed two things. One was that Mom and Ava were now staring at me with shocked expressions. And two, even after two drinks, I still could not smell the delicious blood I had just happily sucked down. I quickly sat the glass down even though I really wanted to finish off its contents and ask for a refill.

"Luke, is that what I think it is?" Mom asked.

"I'm afraid so," I said a little ashamed.

I knew I never would have taken a drink had I known what I was doing. That made me think again about why I couldn't smell it. I suddenly wondered why Mom hadn't smelled it either.

"Why can't I smell it?" Mom asked answering my question.

"I can't smell it either," I told her.

As if on cue, the waiter entered the room. I wasted no time asking him what was going on.

"Why would you serve my son blood?" Mom asked in the fighting tone mothers get when someone has done their child terribly wrong.

The waiter stared at her blankly not knowing what he had done wrong. We always serve blood to the Stallings," he answered. "We have strict orders, ma'am. And, it comes from the youngest donors in the world, just as Mr. Stallings ordered."

"Why can't we smell it?" I asked him before Mom could snap at the innocent man again. I wasn't mad at the man for bringing the blood, he was completely innocent. I secretly wished he would bring me another fresh glass. I had never tasted anything so amazing in all my life.

"Mr. Stallings has it processed before it comes here. I was not aware that it had no smell.

I suddenly became curious about the kinds of things my grandfather's scientists were working on. I was certain he did something to it to remove it's smell. The question in my head now was why?

"The food was absolutely wonderful, sir. Can we please get our check?" I asked him.

"There is no check, sir," the waiter told me. I guess owning the place definitely had its perks.

I made sure to leave a large tip lying on the table when we left. Our car was waiting on us when we made it outside the restaurant. Thomas opened the door and we climbed in.

It was getting pretty late by the time we made it back to the apartment. We noticed Dakota bent over looking in the refrigerator as we came in. I had completely forgot about inviting him to dinner. That was before I knew they served blood. Mom went to bed and left Ava and I up alone with Dakota.

"Hey buddy," I said to Dakota.

"What's up?" He asked. I noticed a bottle sitting on the counter and a glass stained with blood sitting beside it. I guessed Dakota had found Alexander's stash.

"Not much. We were just going to head to bed too. Sorry to leave you up all by yourself.

"Ah, don't worry about it, Luke. I have a couple friends here that I haven't seen in a very long time. I am going to hang out with them for the night. I didn't want to leave before I told you where I was," Dakota explained.

"That's great!" I said, glad he had people he know close by. I wondered who they were, and how he knew them, but it really wasn't any of my business. I stole a glance at the bottle sitting on the counter. I realized there was no smell again and knew it was the same stuff I had drank at the restaurant. "Well, good night then," I told him.

I took Ava by the hand and led her through my room and out onto the balcony. I stood behind her with my arms around her waist and my chin resting on her shoulder. My mind suddenly went back to the amazing flavor of my first drink of blood and the surge of power it sent through my body. I wondered what my family and friends would think knowing I actually enjoyed drinking blood now. I wasn't even sure what I thought about myself because of it.

"This is absolutely amazing, Luke. Thank you so much for inviting me to come along."

"I wouldn't have it any other way. I couldn't stand to be away from you for any length of time."

I was telling the truth. I didn't feel that I could stand a single day away from her. I was so in love with Ava that I could only think of one possible thing to do.

"What would you say if I asked if you would like for all of this to be yours one day?" I whispered into her ear. I immediately felt her body go rigid and could hear her heart start to beat very fast.

"What are you saying, Luke?" she asked after she slowly turned around to look me in the face.

"Well, I love you more than any man could ever love a woman. I want all of this to be yours. I know we are still young, but I want to know if you would like to spend the rest of our lives together." I watched as tears began to form in Ava's eyes as she looked up at me.

"Oh, Luke, I would love more than anything to spend our lives together." The tears began to roll down her cheek and I bent down and put my lips to hers. We kissed for several seconds before she pulled back and looked at me again.

"How can we be together with the supernatural law banning it?" Ava asked.

I really had never thought about that before. I knew Mom and my father had done it, but what consequences had they faced for breaking the law? I would definitely need to find out from her about that, but I refused to let anything or anybody stand in the way of marrying the woman I loved.

"We will cross that bridge when we get to it," I told her.

"I love you so much, Luke," she said as silent tears continued to fall down her cheeks.

"I love you too, Ava," I told her as I bent down to kiss her again.

6

The next morning Mom came into my knocked on my door to wake me up. I didn't know what time it was but I was instantly relieved when I realized I hadn't dreamed about the silver haired creature again.

"What time is it?" I asked groggily.

"It's eight o'clock. Somebody put a letter under the door this morning that said we were due at the attorneys office by nine."

"Mom, I really need to ask you something. Please don't get upset or angry until I finish," I told her as I opened the door and invited her in.

"I could never be angry with you, baby. Is something the matter?" she asked quite concerned as I closed the door behind her.

"Well, you know Ava and I have been dating for a couple years now."

"Of course. You two are wonderful together," she said smiling at me as she took a seat on the edge of my bed.

"I love Ava more than anything. I know we are still pretty young, but I told her last night before we went to bed that I wanted us to spend the rest of our lives together," I told Mom. I waited for a terrible reaction that I felt was coming.

"That is great news, honey. I think the two of you would make a lovely couple. Why would you think I would be angry about that?" she asked curiously.

"Well, that leads me to what I need to ask you. How did you and my father get around the Supernatural laws that forbid two different species from being together?"

"Ah I see. You are worried about getting in trouble with the Council."

"Of course I am. I am, after all, working to enforce the laws. How would it look if I were to go out and break one myself?"

"The Council doesn't forbid races from loving each other and getting married. We found that out when your grandfather decided to turn us in. My father hated that I was with your Dad. He did everything he could to keep us apart. When he found out we were getting married he called the Council and had us brought up before them. They told us that the law states two separate species are not allowed to have children. It says nothing about different species getting married," Mom explained.

"So, as long as we don't plan to have children we will be ok?" I asked her excitedly. It was wonderful to find out we could actually get married. I didn't even think twice about the no children part.

"That's right, baby. Surely you two are not already talking about having children," Mom said more as a statement than a question.

"No! Not at all, Mom. We're not really even old enough to get married yet."

"That is true," she said smiling at me. She kissed me on the forehead before she got up and headed toward the door. "Get up and get ready, Luke. We don't have long before we need to go downstairs."

I was so excited to find out Ava and I could get married. I would have to talk to her about the children issue, but we really didn't have time for kids anyway with all the fighting evil and everything. I got up and took a quick shower before putting on one of the new suits Ava and I had bought at the mall. I didn't know how to tie a tie. I couldn't remember ever wearing one before. I hoped Mom knew how or I would have to go without one.

Ava was already up and dressed by the time I came out of my room. She was absolutely beautiful in one of the formal outfits we also bought at the mall.

"Mom, do you know how to tie one of these darn things?" I asked as I walked over and gave Ava a kiss. "I have something to tell you, but it will have to be a surprise later," I whispered in her ear. She giggled and kissed me again.

"Come here and I'll see what I can do."

Mom tied up my tie like a professional. I guessed she had done it before a time or two.

"My handsome little business man," Mom said. I was used to her calling me baby, but the business man comment made me blush.

I heard Ava giggle again and gave her a funny but evil look. She smiled at me and I smiled back and stuck my tongue out at her.

"Ok, I guess I'm ready. Let's get this show on the road." I don't know why I was so nervous. I was going to sign the papers that would give me an unbelievable amount of money, property, and who knew what else. I still couldn't comprehend how all of this was happening to a kid like me.

We left the apartment headed down to the seventeenth floor. We came off the elevator to be greeted by a young woman behind a desk.

"Do you have an appointment?" The lady asked us.

"Yes. I'm Lucas Stallings. We have an appointment with Mr. Jackson and Mr. Simms," I told her. I watched as the woman picked up the phone and put it to her ear.

"Mr. Stallings is here to see you," she said, "They will see you now." The woman stood up and motioned for us to follow her. We walked to the end of a hall and through a set of double doors.

"Luke. It's a pleasure to see you again," said Mr. Jackson.

"Good morning, Luke," said Mr. Simms.

"Good morning," I replied. I was suddenly very nervous after seeing all of the paperwork stacked in different piles all over the table in front of us.

"Are you ready to get started?" asked Mr. Jackson. "We have a lot to go over."

"As ready as I'll ever be," I said smiling.

"First let's go through the real estate properties that Alexander owned. First is this building that we are in now. This was Alexander's main center of operation. He conducted most all of his business from here. He lived in the penthouse. His office was one floor below, and his research facility is down in the basement. You have two keys that I gave you yesterday. Here is a third key that goes to Alexander's office." explained Mr. Jackson.

"Yes, sir," I said.

"Next is the castle property. Here are the keys to that property as well," said Mr. Jackson.

He handed me a key chain that was labeled "castle." There were several keys attached to it. He continued to tell me about individual properties. With each property he described there was a corresponding set of documents for me to sign, as well as a set of keys. I was underage so my mother had to sign with me as my legal guardian. I had a serious case of writers' cramp by the time I finished signing all of the forms. There were nearly fifty properties all over the country that I had to sign for.

"Ok, all of the properties we just went over are rental properties. That means they have tenants that pay monthly rent or a yearly lease to you for them. Your secretary that works in the office upstairs can go over all of the details with you about that. I will introduce you to her when we tour the rest of this building. Next, we need to go over the businesses that Alexander owned. The rental properties are the first business. The second one is the restaurant where you had dinner last night," Mr. Jackson explained.

Each business also had its own set of keys, and documents for me to sign. All together there were twenty-two businesses including the rental properties and the restaurant. The businesses, much like the real estate, were located all over the world. "Your secretary can answer any questions you may have about the businesses as well."

Each of the documents I signed had two copies that Mom and I had to sign. One was for the attorneys, and one was for my own records. My stack of paperwork was growing thicker by the minute.

"Next we have the issue of Mr. Stallings' bank accounts. The total amount that we have calculated from all of his accounts is this," Mr. Jackson said as he pushed a piece of paper over to me with a large number written on it. I counted nine zeroes after the number in front and immediately realized I wasn't a billionaire. I was actually not sure what to call it with the long list of numbers I was looking at. My heart began to beat fast as the realization of what I was doing kicked in. There were a total of eight different bank accounts that I now signed the documents to take possession of. I added my copies of the documents to the pile.

"The last thing I have for you, before I turn you over to Mr. Simms, is the issue with Alexander's investment portfolio. I have the documents here for you to take full possession of the items at hand. However, you will have to talk to your investor about the details of each one," Mr. Jackson told me.

I was suddenly beginning to get a little overwhelmed. He was telling me about all these different things and I didn't know most of what he was even talking about. I knew I was going to have to get Grandpa to help me with all of this.

"Your secretary can set up a meeting with your investor whenever you get a chance to talk to him. I will now turn you over to Mr. Simms so he can go over your father's business items with you," said Mr. Jackson as he began to smile at me. I knew he could see my very shocked expression. "Everything will be alright, Luke. Know that we will continue to be your attorneys as long as you will have us. We are here for you anytime you need us. Anything at all that you need feel free to call us."

"Luke, your father of course had the money that I told you about. He also had two businesses in the U.S. that he was a joint partner in," said Mr. Simms. I signed the documents for the bank accounts that my father owned. There were two accounts in England and one back home in Little Rock.

"The two businesses are actually at the same location. One of the businesses is the rental of office space in the building itself. The second is a private club located inside the building.

Your business partner is a Mr. Simmons I believe. Yes. Jonathan Simmons was Terry's partner in these businesses," Mr. Simms explained.

My heart sank with this information. Why would my father be partners with the head of the Little Rock vampire coven? I asked myself. I saw Ava looking at me questioningly. I knew she was probably wondering the same thing. There were documents for me to sign for the two businesses in Little Rock as well.

"I believe that concludes the business we have for you, Luke. Do you have any questions for us?" asked Mr. Johnson.

"I don't think so. This is just a lot to take in at one time," I told them.

"Why don't we take a break and have some lunch before we go on a tour of the building," said Mr. Simms.

That definitely sounded like a good idea to me. Mom and Ava agreed. Mr. Jackson told us he had ordered lunch for us and called out to the front desk for the receptionist to bring it in. I finished eating and asked where the restroom was located. I headed down the hall to where Mr. Simms told me it was. Ava caught up to me before I made it there.

"Luke. What do you think about Jonathan and your father being in business together?" Ava asked me.

"I don't really know, but I can't wait to get back and talk to him about it. He never mentioned knowing my father. I guess we will just have to wait and see," I said.

Ava gave me a hug before she headed into the women's restroom. After lunch we headed down to the basement. This was where my grandfather's research facility was located. I didn't have any idea what type of research they did. Neither of the attorneys had mentioned it. Mr. Jackson introduced me to the head of the research and development department.

"Luke, this is Mr. Jameson. He oversees everything that goes on here at the research facility. Any questions you have can be answered by him. This is a restricted area so you will have to go on without us. When Mr. Jameson is finished with you meet us back up at our office and we will take you up to your office to introduce you to Helen," Mr. Jackson told me. He and Mr. Simms headed back up the elevator and left us alone with Mr. Jameson.

"Mr. Stallings, it is a pleasure to meet you. Please call me Walter," The man said.

Walter was an older man. I guessed him to be in his mid to late sixties from the short gray beard and mustache. His head was mostly bald in the front and on top of his head. Short gray hair covered the sides and back. He spoke without an accent, so I assumed he wasn't from England either I suddenly wondered why my grandfather was even set up in England. Not even he was originally from there.

"You can call me Luke," I told him nervously.

I didn't know what to expect from him or this research facility he was about to show me. He led us out of his office and down a long corridor. There were several other offices that he told me belonged to the scientists that worked here. We were nearly to the end of the hall before we actually entered through one of the doors.

The room we entered was solid white from floor to ceiling. There were several work stations that looked like something you would see in a chemistry classroom with test tubes and burners and things cluttering each one. Walter explained the scientists were working on a number of different serums for supernatural creatures. I realized that Walter must know about the supernatural world like the attorneys. I guessed in order to work for a supernatural being you had to know about their world.

One of the serums in particular that Walter said they were working on caught my interest. He said they were working on a serum that would allow vampires to go out into the sunlight. I asked him if they were having any luck with it. He said they did have some success. The combination they came up with so far allowed vampires to go out for only a few minutes at a time. The test subjects that agreed to use it knew the risks, but they were willing to try. The longest experiment, he told us, was three minutes. They couldn't seem to extend the length any longer than that. They had been working on it for several years now. My guess was that vampires had been trying for centuries to come up with something like it. Sunlight, I knew, was a vampires' greatest weakness. I wondered what would happen if vampires could actually run around, and hunt, during the day.

Next Walter took us across the hall. This room was much the same as the first. The difference was, there was only one person working in here. Equipment and supplies littered all of the work surfaces in this room. It was so clustered that I wondered how anybody was able to find anything in all the mess.

"This is actually my work area. I am a weapons designer. I designed weapons for the U.S. government for fifteen years before I came to work for your grandfather," said Walter. That explained the absence of an English accent. He was actually an American. "I have worked for Alexander for about sixteen years now I guess. I hope that I can continue working for you, Luke."

"I never knew Alexander, but if he felt you were an adequate employee I want argue with his judgment," I told him. I didn't trust the Stalling side of my family, but if he trusted these people to work for him they probably were ok. Only time would tell.

"Your grandfather was a great man, and it was definitely my pleasure to work for him. He talked about you all the time. He hoped only for the opportunity to get to know you."

"Then why did he and my father try to lure me here. My father only created me to help him take over the world. I really don't think he wanted to just get to know me."

"Oh, Luke, please don't let your father's actions influence your views about Alexander. Your grandfather had no control over Terry. Normally a vampires' sire, or father, has complete control over their children. Vampires usually respect their fathers enough to obey them. Your father, on the other hand, had no respect for anybody. I assure you. Your grandfather loved you very much, Luke. He was so proud of the man you are turning out to be," explained Walter.

I stared at Walter completely shocked by what he was saying. I didn't know if I could trust what he was telling me or not. I felt horrible about Alexander's death if what Walter was saying was in fact true.

"So, what types of weapons are you working on?" I asked him trying to change the subject.

"Well, I haven't really been working on any weapons for several years. I have mainly been working on a vehicle of sorts," Walter said.

"What kind of vehicle? Like a car?" I asked curiously.

"Not exactly. I have been designing an aircraft that travels at super speed. I believe it is nearly ready for testing. If it works correctly a person would be able to travel from here to the U.S. in just under an hour."

"Wow. That is fast."

"Yes it is," Walter laughed, "The problem I have run into is trying to build it so that anyone can fly it. I'm trying to design it so you don't have to be a pilot in order to operate it. I have just about come up with a way for it to act as a sort of elevator. Instead of going up and down though, it will go from place to place. I think it is almost ready to be tested."

"That's cool. I can't wait to try it out myself."

Walter smiled at me. I could see Mom giving me an evil look at the thought of me flying something that moved so fast.

"That's the research facility as a whole, Luke. Do you have any questions?"

"Not right now. I have had so much thrown at me today that I can't really think straight," I said giggling.

"Feel free to come down here anytime. And, if you ever need anything you can always call me," Walter said handing me a business card. I stuck it in my pocket so I could store it in my phone later.

We headed back upstairs to the attorneys office. Mr. Jackson escorted us up to the floor below the penthouse that was now my office. He introduced me to Helen, my secretary. Helen was an older lady. She reminded me a lot of Grandma. Helen explained that this floor had lots of offices that were not being used. She said Alexander only used his office and she worked at the front desk.

I was exhausted from all of the "business" I had done that day. I told Helen I would come down first thing in the morning and she could discuss Alexander's business with me. She said she would be happy to. Mom, Ava, and I headed up to the penthouse to relax for a while before we went out for dinner.

I had so much to think about I really just wanted to be alone for a while. I told them I was going to take a nap and headed for my room. Mom followed me in and closed the door. I sat down on the bed and she walked over to sit down beside me.

"What's wrong, Mom?" I asked.

"Luke, I wanted to talk to you about Alexander. I knew him and your father didn't get along. When Walter told us about him downstairs it confirmed a lot of things I felt over the years. I really think he was telling the truth about him. Alexander was the only one that accepted your father's and my relationship. I always felt like he loved me even more than his own son," Mom explained.

"So you think my grandfather actually cared about me? You don't think he wanted me because of my power?" I asked puzzled by what she was telling me.

"I think he did, Luke. After hearing what Walter had to say I honestly think he did." I was astounded. The grandfather I allowed to be killed actually had nothing to do with my father's evil schemes.

7

Mom left the room after we talked for a while. I cried for several minutes while thinking about the possibility of Alexander's death being unnecessary. I fell asleep still crying a little. I woke up actually feeling a bit refreshed. I woke up immediately thinking about what all I needed to do about my businesses. I didn't know if I would ever get used to the idea of having multi-million dollar businesses.

I walked out of my room and found Mom and Ava watching TV.

"Hey, Luke. Did you have a good nap?" asked Ava.

"I slept really well, actually," I told her. I walked over and sat down. I had some ideas that I wanted to talk to them about. I wanted to get someone else's opinion. "I have been thinking about something. You know I am supposed to fight evil all over the world, right?"

"Yes. That is what the prophecies say, Luke," Mom said.

"Well, I have been thinking that all of this money and real estate couldn't have come at a better time."

"What do you mean, Luke?" asked Ava.

"I was thinking it would be a great idea to have a headquarters that the Silent Soldiers could use here in England. That way, if something were to happen on this side of the world, we would have a place to stay and work from."

"I think that is a wonderful idea. What did you have in mind, baby?" Mom asked.

"I'm thinking about using the castle for a new headquarters site. What if we were to do some remodeling so we could use it for that purpose? I have been thinking about talking to Eric about moving his pack there to watch over it. He works from home anyway, so it shouldn't be a problem. He mentioned how his pack was starting to outgrow the house they are in anyway. And, if Walter's new aircraft really works the way he said, we could be here in less than an hour if we needed to. I think it would give us a whole new set of eyes and ears in this part of the world. " I explained.

"Luke, I think that is a brilliant idea," said Ava.

"I agree. I am so very proud of you for using your inheritance for the greater good," said Mom.

"I think we should call Grandpa. He should come here and help up plan for this project. I also want to call Eric and see if he can meet with us as well," I told them. We should meet at the castle tomorrow after I finish the business with Helen at the office," I told them.

"Great job honey. It sounds like you have things all lined out. Let me know if there is anything I can do to help," said Mom.

I told them I needed to make a few phone calls. I went out to the balcony and called Eric first. He agreed to come and I told him my plane would pick him up at the airport in London the next day.

Next I called Grandpa.

"Hello?" Grandpa said after the first ring. It seemed as though he was waiting on my phone call.

"Hi, Grandpa, I was wondering if I could talk to you about something very important," I said.

I told him all about my plans for a second headquarters and about asking Eric to move his pack in at the castle to watch over it. I also asked if he would come and meet with us. I told him I would appreciate it if he could come to my office with me the next morning to help me go over my various businesses.

"Luke, I would be honored to help you. I will leave immediately. I should be there sometime in the morning," he said.

"Actually, why don't you let me send my plane. It flies a lot faster. It will only take you five hours to get here," I said.

"Wow that's really fast. I will see you in the morning, Luke. Thank you again for calling me," he said.

Grandpa was acting really weird for some reason. Before we left he kept reminding me I could call him if I needed anything. Now he was thanking me for calling him. Who else did he think I would call? I called Grady and told him the flight plans to bring Grandpa and then pick up Eric from London.

After making my calls I went back out into the room with Mom and Ava. The smell of Chinese food before entering, and the familiar white take out boxes after, I knew it was going to be Chinese for dinner. After dinner both girls decided to go to bed. Neither of them had taken a nap earlier like I had.

I text Dakota and asked what he was up to. He was out with his friends again, so I was left alone for the rest of the night. I walked over to the fridge to get a soda. I immediately noticed the wine bottle from the night before sitting on one of the shelves. I looked around as if somebody might be watching before grabbing the bottle and a glass from the cabinet. I quietly made my way to my room and out onto the balcony. I sat the bottle on the table as I took a seat and looked out over the city. I thought for a while about how much my life had changed over the last few years as I poured a glass of the amazing red liquid I was dying to taste again. I quickly downed the entire glass. I couldn't seem to get enough. I can hardly put into words the delicious flavor that rolled heavily over my tongue.

I woke up sometime around dawn. It was daylight, but the sun had yet to come up. When my eyes opened I had no idea where I was for a split second. I had fallen asleep in the chair on the balcony. It's funny, I didn't even remember falling asleep. The last thing I remember was oh, yeah, I glance over to the now empty bottle and blood stained glass sitting beside me. What was wrong with me? It was like I couldn't control myself once I got started. I honestly wished there was some left in the bottle so I could have another glass.

I suddenly became angry with myself. The thought of drinking somebody's blood should make me sick, but if it tasted anything like what I was drinking from a bottle, I could understand why vampires would want to get it straight from the source. This made me even angrier that I could even think about something like that. I was so ashamed of what was happening to me. I knew it was natural instinct for a vampire to want to feed, but I have never felt the urges I am feeling now.

I feel the need to get rid of the evidence. I didn't want anybody to find out about what I had done. I stood up and looked down over the edge of the balcony. I spotted a dumpster a couple blocks over. I took aim a threw the bottle as hard as I could. It flew threw the air for several seconds before hitting its target. The bottle hit the inside of the dumpster so hard it actually moved the dumpster a few feet. Wow! I thought to myself. I realized I had never really tested out my powers before.

I jumped in the shower and got dressed for the day. I had told Mom and Ava they could sleep in. I knew they would be bored having to listen to Helen tell me all about the endless list of businesses and bank accounts that I now owned. I made it to the office at nine like I told Helen I would the day before.

"Good morning, Mr. Stallings. Can I get you some coffee or something to eat?" asked Helen.

"Call me Luke. And, I don't really drink coffee but something to eat and a soda would be great," she said.

She showed me to my grandfather's office before making a phone call to order food. Apparently there was some kind of snack shop that rented a space on the first floor. I began to look through Alexander's desk drawers while I waited for my food to arrive.

The last drawer I tried to open was locked. Helen had given me a set of keys before she left and told me they were to the office and the filing cabinets. I started trying each one until the drawer finally opened.

There were several file folders in this drawer. The one that immediately caught my attention was labeled "Lucas". I immediately pulled it out and laid it on the desk. I nervously opened the folder to see what was inside. The folder was filled with large close-up photos of me. Surprisingly the photos were from all different ages of my childhood. Some of them went as far back as when I was just a toddler. How did Grandpa get pictures of me when I was in hiding with Uncle Charles? Did he know where I was the whole time? I was shocked and confused by what I was seeing.

I began to smell the familiar fragrance of bacon and eggs and knew breakfast must have arrived. I could hear the click of Helen's heels on the tile floor coming down the hall. I closed the folder and shoved it back in the drawer just as she began to knock.

"Come in," I said.

Helen brought in a container and a can of soda and sat it on the desk in front of me. "Is there anything else I can get for you?" she asked.

"Thank you, Helen. I think that will be all for now," I said. My phone began to ring as she headed out the door. It was Grandpa. They were close to landing at the airport. He asked me where he was supposed to go. I told him my car would be waiting for him. I hung up the phone and quickly dialed Thomas's number. He told me he would go immediately.

I had brought my backpack with my laptop in it. I quickly pulled the folder back out of the drawer and shoved it in with my laptop. I continued looking through the rest of the file cabinets in the office waiting for Grandpa to arrive. I had no idea what I was really looking at with all of the business language they contained. That is exactly why I wanted Grandpa to come help me.

"Luke, a Mr. Carrington is here to see you," Helen said over the intercom on the desk.

"Please send him in," I said when I finally figured out what button to push to answer her. Grandpa walked in a minute later with a huge smile on his face.

"Good morning, Luke," he said as he came over and gave me a huge hug.

"Morning, Grandpa. I am so happy you're here. I have no idea what all of this stuff is. Helen is going to come in and go over the various businesses I now own. After that I can show you the documents from my different properties."

"Slow down buddy!" Grandpa said laughing.

I guess I didn't realize I had gotten a little excited and carried away. I was just happy that Grandpa was finally here. It scared me to know that I was now in charge of a huge empire that my grandfather created over hundreds of years as a vampire.

Grandpa and I went into a large conference room where we listened as Helen explained everything she knew about Alexander's business. Helen left to return to her duties in the front office. She told me she was available anytime should any questions arise. Grandpa looked through several of the files in silence. From time to time he would try to explain some of the things he was reading. I was beginning to get an overall idea of how Alexander ran his operation.

Just then Helen announced that Eric had arrived. I told her to send him in.

"Good evening, Eric. I am glad you could join us," I told him as I stood to shake his hand. I had only met Eric a short time ago, but I knew he was a guy I could trust and I liked him a lot.

"It's a pleasure to see you again, Eric," said Grandpa.

"Thank you for having me. To what do I owe the pleasure of this meeting?" asked Eric.

"Let's go back to my office and I will try to explain some ideas I have. I think they can greatly benefit all of us," I told them. I had been thinking about several ideas I had for a second headquarters location. The first hurdle I needed to cross would be getting Eric to agree to move his pack to the castle.

"Eric, I have a business proposition for you. I know you have business of your own, but I think I can solve the housing problem you mentioned as well as generate a sizable income for your pack."

"You definitely have my attention, Luke. What do you have in mind?" asked Eric. I began to explain my idea to Grandpa and Eric about having a second headquarters. I told them it would allow us to have eyes and ears on both sides of the world. I told Eric I would put him and the members of his pack on my payroll to operate and protect the new facility. I told them my plans to convert the castle for this purpose.

"That sounds like a marvelous idea, Luke. We would love to help you and the soldiers any way we can. My only concern is the length of time it takes to get to the castle. It definitely would not be convenient for the pack members that work in the city," said Eric.

"I believe I have a solution for that as well," I said. I began to tell them what I had learned about the properties. "The land surrounding the property is several thousand acres. We could build a small airstrip big enough to land a plane the size of mine and yours, Grandpa. I could leave you my plane. You can fly your pack back and forth to the city if you need to. Or, the ones that live in the city can stay at they house you have there now. They can come to the castle on their free time.

After some time Eric agreed to discuss the matter with his pack. He said he would let me know their decision by morning. He left the office headed back to London. I became nervous as to whether Eric and his pack would even want to move way out there. I guessed we would just have to wait and see what they decided. Grandpa now sat before me smiling.

"You seem to be adjusting to your new position quite well," he said.

"Grandpa, you have no idea how nervous I am about all of this. I don't have a clue about how to run a business, especially as big as the one I now have. That is why I called you to help. I also called you to see if I could hire you to oversee the project at the castle. I know you did all of the work for headquarters at the mansion, and I wanted your expertise for this to be a success," I said.

"Luke, you know I will help you in any way I can. I don't expect any kind of payment for helping. I have dedicated my life, and the lives of my pack members, to serving the Silent Soldiers. I consider this to be part of that dedication. I am just so proud of you for coming up with the idea," he said.

"Well, if we are going to save the world we definitely can't do it all from Eerie!" I said laughing.

"Well, Luke, your Grandma and I were wondering what the next part of the prophecy meant," said Grandpa.

"What do you mean Grandpa?"

"The prophecy says the white wolf creates an empire to protect the world from evil."

"Oh. I guess that means we are on track then right?" I asked.

"I would say the Silent Soldiers are definitely heading in the right direction," said Grandpa.

I saw the familiar look as Grandpa stared back at me smiling. I knew Grandpa was very proud of the man I was turning into. I loved to make Grandpa happy, and I could tell I had succeeded with all of the plans I had come up with for the new headquarters location. But, he had no idea what plans I had in store for the future.

8

Grandpa worked through the files in my office for the next two days. I had learned a lot about the various operations within the businesses Alexander had created. We had a construction company working day and night putting in the small runway close to the castle. By the weekend they called to let us know it was finished enough for us to land my plane there. We decided to stay at the castle for the weekend to come up with a plan for the renovations.

I called Grady to make arrangements for him to fly us to the castle that afternoon. Next, I called Thomas and told him I needed him to run an errand. I needed him to pick something up before we headed to the castle. I had promised Ava a surprise and I wanted to do it soon. When I got back to the penthouse everyone was ready to go. I grabbed the things I would need and we headed to the airport.

Eric and his pack had decided to go forward with the invitation I offered them. He and a few of his pack members met us at the airport. They were going with us to the castle to take part in our planning. I knew Eric, and I recognized the other two men he brought along with him as two of the shifters that helped with the battle at the castle against my father. The only person I didn't know was the young girl that Eric introduced as his daughter.

"This is my sister, Katie. She is an electronics genius," Eric said, "She is going to help us with setting up the networks and surveillance systems for the new headquarters." I thought Katie was a bit young to be a "genius" of any kind, but if Eric said she was I definitely trusted him. She appeared to be a year or two younger than me. She was a little shorter than Ava with sandy blonde hair. She seemed quite shy and didn't say much on the way to the castle.

I stood on the new airstrip after landing at the castle and was amazed at the work they had accomplished in such a short time. The runway was completed, and the framework for a large hangar was already in place. I knew they would be finished with it in another day or two. Grandpa had mentioned we needed a vehicle that could carry us to and from the castle, so he and I had ordered one the day before. I now noticed a large black hummer, already outfitted with the Silent Soldiers logo, parked a short distance from the plane. We loaded our things into the back and headed off toward the castle.

When we got to the castle Mom showed us around. She showed us the bedrooms upstairs where we each picked a room and put our things away. I told Eric he could go ahead and occupy the master suite. It was going to be his when the pack moved in anyway. Grandpa, Eric, and the pack members that accompanied him set off on a tour of the first floor to start their planning process.

It was beginning to get dark outside by the time we settled in at the castle. I asked Ava if she would like to go for a walk with me. We hadn't been alone in several days and we needed some time to ourselves for a change. We set out around the wall surrounding the castle. We were nearly around to the back of the castle before Ava stopped and pulled me around to stand in front of her.

"So what is this surprise you told me about? I have been waiting for several days now." She said.

I had been so busy working with Grandpa that I hadn't really had time to talk to Ava at all. I pulled her close and gave her a kiss. Suddenly I saw something move just inside the edge of the woods. I instinctively pulled Ava around behind me as I searched the area closely looking for the source of the movement.

"Do you see that?" I asked.

"See what? I can't really see in the dark, Luke."

"Right there around the bottoms of those trees. It looks like tiny little people running back and forth between those trees." I said.

"I don't see anything." She said. I took Ava by the hand and started walking toward the movement. We were nearly to the wood line when I stopped instantly and the muscles in my body clenched. I felt Ava tense as well when she saw what I was looking at. There were dozens of little people running around from tree to tree. They appeared to be hiding in the roots of the trees. The little people were no more than a foot tall. They were all chubby with fat little round faces.

The little people were all throwing sticks and rocks in the same direction. The creature they appeared to be fighting off was what stopped Ava and I from going any further. The creature was jet black in color with glowing red eyes. Its teeth were long and pointed and dripped a nasty green colored slime as it snarled and snapped at the tiny little people. The creature was the shape of a very large dog. The difference was that the two legs in the front were much longer than the two in the back. The front legs had razor sharp claws that it kept slashing toward the little people that got too close.

I suddenly realized I needed my sword. In less than three seconds I used my vampire speed to go to my room, grab the sword, and return to Ava's side. She never even knew I left her. When she looked over and realized I was now transformed into my white uniform I heard her gasp. I jumped into the air, in vampire speed, pulling my sword from its sheath. When I came down I slashed in a downward motion landing beside the mean dog looking creature. The creature's head fell to the ground and its lifeless body followed shortly after. A nasty green colored liquid oozed from its neck where the head was no longer attached.

There was a few seconds of silence before loud cheering and applause erupted from behind me. I glanced back and noticed the cheering was coming from the little people that had been desperately fighting off the creature.

I noticed one of the little people walking shyly toward me. This one seemed to be older than the rest. He was the only one I noticed having a short grayish white beard. He made sure not to get too close before he spoke to me.

"We thank you for saving us from the horrific and troublesome ghoul," said the man.

"What is a ghoul?" I asked.

"That is a ghoul, of course," the man said pointing toward the now dead creature, "This ghoul has plagued our villages for many years. Nobody living at the castle has ever cared enough to protect us. We are forever grateful, and forever in your service young giant," said the little man.

"What are you, exactly?" I asked the little man. I didn't realize how rude I sounded before the words came out of my mouth, but I really wanted to know.

"Please forgive me for not introducing myself. I am Fehren. I am the leader of the colony of gnomes that has protected this castle for centuries," he said. He pronounced his name (Fair-in).

I wondered how a group of tiny creatures could possibly protect the castle by throwing sticks and rocks, but I kept my thoughts to myself.

"I'm Luke, and this is my friend Ava. I am the new owner of the castle. It is a pleasure to meet you, sir," I said. I crouched down on one knee and reached out to shake his hand. The little man jumped back at my sudden movement. "It's ok,

Fehren. I promise I'm not here to hurt anybody. He cautiously walked over and put his hand toward mine. His hand was so small that it was only big enough to wrap around two of my fingers. I gently shook his hand before he took a few steps back away from me.

"What happened to the vampires?" he asked.

"Vampires? What vampires?" I said looking around the woods.

"The vampires that lived in the castle," he said.

"Oh, well, it is a long story," I told him.

"We have all the time in the world," he said. Fehren walked over and hopped up onto a nearby stump and stared at me questioningly. I realized he expected me to tell him what happened. I left out a lot of the details but I told him Alexander had been my grandfather. I told him the vampires at the castle were evil and had been killed. I told him I inherited the castle from them. I didn't want him to know I had anything to do with their deaths. I was surprised they didn't already know if they were protecting the castle.

By the time I finished my story all of the little gnomes had gathered around and were listening closely to what I had to say. "We are at your service, Luke," said Fehren as he jumped down from his seat and bowed toward me.

"Thank you, Fehren. If you ever need my help please don't hesitate to ask me. We can't be having these creatures roaming around the forest," I said.

"I believe the worst is finally over, Luke. You have defeated the gnome's worst enemy," he said. Ava and I said good bye to Fehren and the rest of the gnomes. It was getting pretty late by the time we finished talking to them. We headed back to the castle before Mom decided to send out a search party. I guessed the good news I had for Ava would have to wait.

Just as we made it back to the front of the castle I stopped and turned toward Ava. I didn't know when we would be alone again, and I wasn't going to miss my opportunity for one more private kiss from my beautiful girlfriend. I pulled her close and gently put my lips to hers.

"Luke!" came a loud voice from behind me. My body tensed and I felt Ava jump in surprise to the sudden sound.

"Jordan! What are you doing here?" I asked once I realized who it was. "You're going to get yourself hurt sneaking up on people like that," I told her pointing to the sword on my back.

"Who are you?" asked Ava a little rudely.

I forgot I hadn't already told Ava about Jordan. I quickly brought her up to speed. I guess there was no sense trying to hide it now.

"So, have you made a decision yet?" Jordan asked after I was finished explaining to Ava about her.

"Jordan, I have been so busy I haven't had time to even think about it. I told you before I don't even know HOW to turn anybody even if I wanted to," I explained.

I watched as Jordan hung her head in disappointment. I didn't know why, but I knew Jordan wanted to be a vampire more than anything. How could I convince her it was a terrible idea? Not that it is a bad thing to be a vampire, because I am of course half vampire myself. I suddenly couldn't think of a single reason why Jordan shouldn't be turned. I wondered why it was so important that Jordan wanted me to be the one to turn her. It said a lot that she hadn't already found somebody to do it.

Suddenly I caught a bit of movement out of the corner of my eye. At first I thought it was a gnome playing at the base of a large tree. The movement would never have been noticed by a normal set of eyes. With my recent liking from blood, I had noticed my sight wasn't normal even for a vampire. My powers were definitely getting stronger, especially in the senses department.

I noticed the movement again, this time it came from a different direction. I turned my head quickly realizing that no gnome could ever move over three hundred yards in the blink of an eye. I instantly began to focus on the dark spot. I could tell the creature was small, even at the incredible distance it was from me. But, I couldn't make out any of its features. I suddenly had an uneasy feeling as though we were being watched.

I casually move our little group through the gate and closer to the front door of the castle. I didn't want to alarm the girls, but something didn't feel right. You know the feeling you get just before the hairs stand up on the back of your neck? Well, multiply that by about a hundred and that is how I felt right now.

"Luke, what do I have to do to convince you to turn me?" asked Jordan from behind me. I noticed I had completely turned my back on both of them as I continued to focus on the little dark spot in the wood line.

"Luke, what are you looking at?" asked Ava.

The dark spot suddenly disappeared again. I scanned the edge of the woods back and forth looking for where the spot would turn up next.

"Luke!" Jordan nearly shouted. I was so focused that the sudden outburst made me jump.

"It's probably nothing," I said as I continued to scan the area.

"What do you mean probably nothing?" Ava asked emphasizing the probably part.

"Well, I saw something in the woods, but there is no telling what all lives out there," I said trying to convince myself it was nothing.

"Can we get back to the issue at hand then?" asked Jordan sarcastically? "I'm not getting any younger here!"

I couldn't fight this strange feeling I had. I began to get a little sick to my stomach by it though, and I wanted it to stop.

"Jordan, I really don't know what to tell you. There has got to be some kind of supernatural law about it somewhere," I told her. "Why can't you believe me when I tell you I don't even know how to turn anybody."

"And, who says Luke even wants to turn you?" Ava asked. I noticed the bitter tone in her voice. I appreciated the possessiveness Ava was displaying. I realized even more how much she cared about me. She knew me better than anybody, and she knew I would never even think about hurting somebody.

Suddenly there was a puff of smoke beside us. I instinctively drew my sword in preparation for the expected battle ahead. But, when the smoke cleared I realized it was only Cameron.

"Cam! What are you doing here?" I asked him.

"I felt you were in trouble, Luke. I had to come check on you. I'm sorry if I interrupted something," Cam said nervously. I guess with whatever connection we had, Cam could feel the uneasy sensation I had.

"Hi, Cam!" Ava said excitedly. It is great to see you.

"Hey, Ava," said Cam.

"I hate to break up this little reunion, but actually, you ARE interrupting!" Jordan said.

"Jordan if you are going to be rude to my friends, you can definitely forget about me ever turning you," I said sternly.

I watched as a huge smile spread across Jordan's face. She had been moping around ever since she got here, so I wondered why she was so happy all of a sudden.

"Why are you smiling?" asked Ava.

"I'm just happy that you are actually considering doing the job!" exclaimed Jordan.

"What job?" I asked confused.

"Turning me, silly," Jordan said.

"What exactly gave you that idea?" I asked her.

"You just said if I continue to be rude you wouldn't turn me. So, I definitely want be rude anymore. Jordan walked over and picked up Cam and gave him a big hug to emphasize not being rude."

I didn't like the fact that Jordan seemed to turn my words around on me. I never had any intention of turning her. I guess I should start thinking more before I open my mouth. I didn't press the issue any further. I knew it wasn't going to happen today for sure. Even if I changed my mind about doing it I would have to learn how first.

The events that happened next were so fast that they are nearly just a blur. The first thing I remember happening is the sudden appearance of a familiar purple shield. The same type shield that Jack used to save me and Matt from the vampires at the mansion on the night I shifted for the first time. The purple shield surrounded all four of the people standing in the group.

The next thing that happened was catching movement at the top of the wall surrounding the castle. I stared up in horror at the creature standing on top of it. It was the same silver haired creature that had recently plagued my nightmares. I continued to stare at him in shock. I was frozen with fear as I watched him pull an arrow into the familiar silver handled bow he held in his hand. I willed my body to take action, but nothing would happen. My body was not responding.

The creature released the arrow. I watched the arrow fly through the air as I heard Jordan say, "the dark one," from close by. The arrow made its way toward us and to my surprise flew right threw Cam's purple shield. My instincts kicked in when I realized who the target was for the creatures' arrow. With my super speed I was in front of the arrow long before it had time to reach Ava.

I quickly reached up to grab hold of the arrow in mid air, but I was too late. I caught the arrow, but not before it pierced the skin of my left shoulder. I don't know what magical powers the creature put on the arrow, but he had succeeded in learning my only known weakness. The last thing I remember was the uncontrollable scream that escaped my mouth as my body crumbled toward the ground. I blacked out before I hit the ground.

9

When I came to for the first time another uncontrollable scream erupted from the pain in my shoulder. The pain was so bad, unlike anything I ever thought possible. The pain was so terrible that it seemed to radiate throughout my entire body. I instantly blacked out again from it unable to tell where I was or how long I had been out.

I woke up several more times in such pain that I would black out again. I lost count of how many times it happened. I had no sense of anything other than the awful pain. I didn't even have time to think about my friends that were left unprotected against the evil black creature. I eventually came to and noticed the pain had greatly decreased. I blinked several times trying to bring my eyes into focus. I immediately noticed I was in my room at the mansion.

I slowly looked around at the crowd of people that were packed in my room. I noticed Dr. Blevins first, because she was right in my face when I could finally see again.

"Welcome back, Luke. We have definitely been worried about you," she said quietly.

"How long have I been out?" I asked groggily.

"Luke! You're awake!" Ava exclaimed as she raced over to the side of my bed and took my hand in hers. I squeezed it gently as I watched the tears stream down her cheeks.

"It happened a week ago, baby," said Mom. I noticed everyone had begun to crowd around my bed. Matt, Jenna,

Dante, Grandpa, Grandma, and several others. They all smiled happily seeing me finally awake after so many days.

"Where is Cam and Jordan? Are they ok?" What happened after that thing shot me? And, how did it shoot me in the first place?" I began asking all the questions I desperately needed answers to. Nobody seemed to be answering so I sat up quickly. The pain suddenly began to intensify in my shoulder to the point that I was yelling uncontrollably. The pain continued to get worse until I couldn't bear it anymore and I passed out once again.

When I woke up the next time I thought everyone had left me in my room alone. I slowly turned my head and realized Ava was asleep next to me. I reached over with my good arm and brushed the hair from her face. Ava stirred with my slightest of touch and opened her eyes. The pain in my arm was gone, but I didn't want to black out again so I kept it motionless as I watched Ava smile back at me.

"What happened?" I asked her.

"Well, once you collapsed the elf moved nearly as fast as you. Everything happened in the blink of an eye. The elf jumped off the top of the wall and landed between us. He grabbed Cam around the neck and Jordan grabbed a hold of the elf. In an instant, they all disappeared. I was left there standing alone with you on the ground and blood was pouring out of your shoulder. I tried a healing spell, but it didn't work at all," explained Ava.

"Where are they? Did somebody find them?" I asked referring to Jordan and Cam. I suddenly became worried about them as I tried to sit up again. Ava stopped me and told me I needed to rest. She told me I wasn't quite well enough to be moving around yet.

"Jordan has come back several times as she has attempted to follow the elf in search of Cam. Her and Jack are out looking for him right now," said Ava.

"Did you say that thing is an elf? It doesn't look like any elf I have ever seen before. Not that I have seen very many, but that one is definitely different," I told her.

"His name is Bregolien (Brehg-ole-ee-ehn), but Jordan says he goes by the name Devlin," Ava told me. "He is a dark elf that has been known world wide for hundreds of years. That's all we know about him so far."

"We need to get busy trying to find them. We have to save Cam!" I told her excitedly as I once again tried to get up out of the bed.

"Lucas Stallings, if you don't lay down and rest I am going to have to put a spell on you," said Ava.

I looked over and noticed that Ava was smiling at me after she pulled me back down to my pillow again. She didn't know it but she already had a spell on me. I would do anything for her. I proved that to myself by jumping in front of the arrow.

"What is a dark elf?" I asked her curiously.

"Well, Jack says an elf becomes dark when they kill the person they have pledged to protect. What we don't understand is why he would come after somebody he doesn't even know," said Ava.

I had a good idea who was behind the why of this whole scheme, and I was determined to find out exactly why.

"You need to get some rest, Luke. You need to get well and get stronger before you run out and try to save the world," Ava said.

I knew Ava was right, but it didn't help the fact that I hate feeling helpless. There was apparently no way anybody was going to let me go out and try to help save Cam, but I had to think of something.

"I'm really hungry," I said as my stomach growled quite loudly. I realized I hadn't eaten in a week. Ava offered to go downstairs and grab me something to eat. I knew we could just call the kitchen and have something brought up, but I didn't say anything. I needed Ava to leave long enough for me to do a little research on my laptop. When I knew she was far enough away from the door I got up and went into the bathroom. When I turned on the light I was shocked to realize I was completely naked. I became quite embarrassed as I thought about the rather large number of people that could have seen my naked body while I was knocked out for a week. I wondered who was selected to be in charge of removing them in the first place.

Surprisingly my nudity was the first thing I noticed. A few seconds after I got over the shock of being naked, the wound left by the arrow came into focus. I gasped at the gruesome sight. My shoulder was completely black and blue around the wound. The wound itself looked to be big enough to put a baseball inside of it. I was surprised I couldn't see bone. No wonder I had been in so much pain. Around the darkest part of the wound, spider web like veins covered most of the upper part of my body. I went into the closet and threw on the most comfortable clothes I could find and quickly made my way back out to grab my laptop.

When I opened my back pack I immediately noticed the folder I had found in my grandfather's office back in England. I wanted to check it out some more, but I had more important issues to deal with first. I climbed back into my bed and powered up the computer. I waited patiently for the Silent Soldiers database to load. I noticed a new icon on the homepage after logging in called Freak-o-pedia. I clicked on it unable to control my interest in the title. I was fascinated by what I saw on the next page. The new page contained a list of dozens of creatures, some of them I was familiar with like vampires and werewolves, but some I had never even heard of.

As I scrolled down the page one creature in particular caught my attention. I clicked on the tab titled Elf, and began reading. What I learned on the page confirmed what Ava said about elves that kill their charge being turned to darkness. Elves are generally happy, kind, loving creatures. They pledge their lives to protect their charges. I continued to read farther down the page. I learned that when an elf murders their charge for any reason, they are turned to darkness. Everything from their outward appearance to the very person they are changes to evil.

I was so focused on what I was reading, I never heard Ava open the door to my room.

"Luke! What are you doing out of bed?" asked Ava. "You must have thought I was joking about the spell," she added laughing.

"I was naked," I told her as I suddenly became embarrassed again at the thought.

"You shouldn't be getting up so soon. You were nearly killed by that injury and you need to take it easy," she said lovingly.

"I feel fine thought," I lied.

The pain in my shoulder was beginning to get worse. I shut the computer and pushed it to the side as Ava brought a tray of food over and sat it in front of me. I was starving, and wasted no time digging in.

"I saw your Grandpa down in the kitchen. He asked about you. He told me Jack is still on the dark ones trail. He said Cam has been leaving him clues along the way," Ava said as I continued to eat the delicious burger and fries she had brought me.

"You said the dark one. I heard Jordan say the same thing just before I was shot," I said after suddenly remembering.

"Jack says the dark one is famous in the elf world. He said the dark elf is the most evil elf of all time."

"Really? I would have to say I agree with that," I said pointing to the wound on my shoulder.

"He wasn't shooting at you," said Ava.

"What?" I asked. I heard her the first time, but I stalled in order to come up with something good to say in response.

"The dark one was shooting at me. I know you moved in front of me to block the arrow," Ava blurted out. I guessed being subtle about it was out of the question.

"And I would do it again a thousand times if it meant I could save your life," I told her.

"I know you would Luke, and I would do the same for you, but I can't help wondering why he was after me," Ava said.

"That is definitely a question I would like to know the answer to myself. I can't wait to find out who or what is behind this. I will personally be dealing with them when I find out," I said.

Ava continued talking while I finished my lunch or dinner or whatever time of day it was. She told me about the series of events that happened after I was shot. Grandpa had the best doctors and supernatural beings all swarming to England to try and figure out why you weren't healing. In fact, your injury continued to get worse. Finally your after about 4 days you stopped getting worse and slowly started to get better. That's when you first started trying to wake up. Once you were stable your Grandpa had you brought back to the mansion. He felt he could protect you and take better care of you here at home.

"I have so much to do back in England. We never finished going through everything at the office. I really need to get back!" I said.

"Luke, your Grandpa has everything under control. You need to relax and just focus on getting better. We are doing everything we can to find Cam. Everything is under control," Ava said.

I knew she was only trying to comfort me, but I had a ton of things I needed to get done. I also needed to get back to school. I was already a week behind. Who knew how long it would be before I was able to go back.

"Matt and Jenna brought all of your homework for the week. Unfortunately they brought mine as well. We could work on it together if you like," said Ava.

"Maybe we can get started on it in the morning. I am kind of tired, I think I am just going to go to bed," I said.

The pain in my shoulder was getting much worse, and I knew I needed to rest it. I kissed Ava good night and she left for her own room. I got up and walked to the fridge to get something to drink. When I opened the door I was shocked by what I found. Sitting on the top shelf were two bottles of my grandfather's wine bottles. I knew instantly they didn't contain wine. I grabbed my phone and sent Dante a quick message. In a matter of seconds there was a knock at the door.

"It's open!" I said. Dante quickly made his way over to where I was standing at the bar.

"I am glad to see you are feeling better, buddy!" said Dante. "You sure had us scared for a few days. I don't know what was on that arrow, but it sure did mess you up bad."

"Did you put those bottles in my refrigerator?" I asked not beating around the bush about it.

"Of course I did, man. I thought you might want to celebrate once you woke up," said Dante smiling.

"Why would you think I would want to drink that?" I asked him.

"Man you finished off a whole bottle in one night while we were in England. I thought you would like them," he told me.

"I do, man. I just tried so hard to cover up the fact that I had drank it. I kind of got a little freaked out when I realized you knew," I said.

"Your secret is safe with me, Luke. But, I don't really understand why you would want to hide it. It is only natural for a vampire to want it. It's what we live for, after all," said Dante.

I knew Dante was telling the truth, but I couldn't help but feel ashamed about it. What would Ava think or my mom if they knew I was drinking blood? I slowly walked over to the counter and grabbed two glasses. I grabbed a bottle from the fridge and headed back to the bar where Dante waited smiling.

"That's what I'm talking about, Luke!"

"Your right, man. It is only a natural instinct that I would want to drink blood. And it tastes so darn good!" I exclaimed as I tried to open the bottles.

"Mmmm," said Dante after taking a sip from the glass I handed him.

I smiled before turning up my glass and drinking its entire contents. I sat my empty glass on the counter in front of me.

"Slow down there big man. Drinking like that will have you flat on your butt in no time. That is some powerful stuff you're drinking there. You might should pace yourself a little bit," said Dante.

"You talk like its alcohol or something. Its not like I can get drunk drinking blood, right?" I asked curiously.

"Well, not alcohol, but it can give you a similar effect. When a vampire drinks from someone as young as the donors used to make that," Dante said pointing at the bottle sitting between us, "It can put you into a drunk like state. If you're body isn't used to it that is."

I wondered just how young the people were that I had been drinking from. I tried to forget about it because it only made me feel that much worse about drinking it at all. Dante poured us both another glass and again, I downed the contents.

"Ok, don't say I didn't warn you, man," Dante said as he began to laugh.

Suddenly I began to feel a surge of heat going through my chest. It felt so hot I feared my skin would be burned. I looked down and noticed a bright blue light coming from the center of my chest through my shirt. Without thinking I quickly took off my shirt to see exactly where the light was coming from. I was amazed to find out it was coming from the wolf's tooth necklace Ava had given me for my birthday a few years back.

I looked over at Dante as the heat began to radiate throughout my body. I became so light headed I nearly fell over. If the bar had not been right in front of me I probably would have. Just as I begin to think the heat would cook me from the inside out, it disappeared completely, and the light on my chest went out. Dante stared with his mouth hanging open at my left shoulder.

"It's gone!" Dante exclaimed.

"What's gone?" I asked confused.

"Everything, man! You are completely healed!" he said excitedly.

I ran to the bathroom and looked in the mirror. I stared in disbelief at what I was seeing. My shoulder was completely healed. You could no longer even tell where the arrow had been at all. I slowly returned to the bar. I poured another glass of blood and took a sip before I could find any words to say.

"What just happened?" Dante asked.

"Well, I think my necklace just healed me!" I said.

10

I quickly grabbed my cell phone and checked the time. I couldn't believe it was only seven o'clock. I was a little ashamed to have sent Ava away so early. I sent her a quick message and a few minutes later there was a knock at the door.

"Luke! What are you doing out of bed?" Ava asked. "I leave you for a few minutes and you....," Ava trailed off. I noticed she was now staring at my shoulder. She had the same reaction as Dante with her mouth hanging open.

"Surprise!" I said trying to be funny.

"How...," was all Ava could seem to say.

I quickly ran through the story about the events leading up to me being healed. I even told her the part about drinking blood and waited for a terrible reaction.

"Luke, I am so happy you are ok!" Ava exclaimed. I came to the conclusion that she either didn't hear me mention the blood, or she didn't care. Either way I didn't mention it again.

I pulled her close for a hug and lifted her easily off the ground and into my arms. I put my lips to hers.

"And that would be my cue to leave. I would say get a room, but this IS your room," Dante said laughing.

"Aw, you don't have to leave," Ava said.

"Yeah, man. You can stay. We just got a little too excited I guess," I told him. "We need to go down and tell everybody the good news."

We finally found Mom, Grandma, and Grandpa in the great room downstairs. They all nearly went crazy seeing me out of bed and downstairs. They were just as shocked as the rest of us once I showed them my injury was completely healed. Hugs and kisses came from every direction.

"I have to get back to work," I told them once everybody had settled down from the excitement.

"Luke, I think you need to take it easy for a few days," Mom said. I noticed the concern in her voice.

"I know you guys are looking out for me, but I don't need to be babied about this. I have way too much to do to let a little arrow keep me from moving forward. I have to get to work trying to find Cam, and I have to get my business in order in England," I explained to them.

"That little arrow nearly got you killed!" Grandma exclaimed.

"Luke is right!" said Grandpa. Of all the people I thought would support me with this, Grandpa was probably the last one I expected to be on my side. "That is exactly what evil wants is for Luke and the soldiers to be out of commission. I am proud of you for bouncing back so quickly after such a terrible ordeal, Luke," Grandpa said as he walked over and patted me on the back.

Our discussion was cut short as my phone rang in my pocket. I quickly pulled it out and realized it was Walter from my lab in England.

"Hello?" I said kind of puzzled. I wondered why he was calling me.

"Mr. Stallings, I wanted to tell you straight away that the final testing for the transportation pods I told you about is complete. They are ready!" Walter exclaimed excitedly.

"That is great news Walter. I will be back soon and you can show me how to use it," I told him.

I said goodbye to Walter and realized everybody was looking at me. I told them all about the pods Walter had been working on. I noticed the amazement Grandpa showed in his expression. Even as young as I was, I knew this invention could change the way people travel forever.

"I need to run an errand tonight, but I plan to leave first thing in the morning if anybody wants to go with me to the castle," I said. I wasn't asking for permission, and hoped that none of my adult family members were going to get upset by my boldness. I noticed Ava smiling at me and knew she wanted to be at my side for the return trip. "Once we get these pods in operation we can travel from here to the castle in an hour," I said trying to lighten the mood.

"I'll be happy to go with you, Luke," said Grandpa. I was definitely happy he was going with me. I needed his expertise when it came to the business side of things. I had an empire to create according to the prophecy and I intended to start first thing in the morning.

Nobody asked what kind of errand I had to run, so Ava and I dismissed ourselves and headed toward headquarters.

"Where are we going?" Ava asked once we were out of the great room.

"I need to go see Jonathan. I want to find out if there is anything he can do to help find Cam. I want you to stay here and get your things ready to go in the morning. I'm not taking you in the middle of a vampire coven again. It was way too uncomfortable last time," I told her.

"Ok, Luke. Please be careful. I'll see you when you get back," Ava said. I was glad she didn't sound disappointed. I hoped she realized I only had her safety in mind by not wanting her to come with me.

Once I was on the highway I started to realize that my senses were extremely heightened. The speedometer said I was going a hundred and forty miles an hour, but the world around me seemed to be sitting still. In a matter of minutes I was pulling into the parking lot behind Jonathan's building. Well, actually since I took over my fathers businesses, I guessed I was part owner of the building as well.

For the first time there was zero trouble as I made my way to Jonathan's office. He was sitting behind his desk with his feet propped on top of it grinning from ear to ear.

"What's up bro? Long time no see!" Jonathan exclaimed.

"It's been a while hasn't it?" I asked.

"We thought you didn't like us anymore or something, bro." Jonathan said. I suddenly wondered why he kept calling me bro. He sounded like one of those stoned out surfer dudes you see in the movies.

"I came to ask you for a favor," I told him.

"Anything for my little bro," said Jonathan.

"Why do you keep calling me bro?" I finally decided to ask him.

"Well, I recently found out that we have the same dad!" Jonathan said excitedly. "So, that makes you my little brother."

"What are you talking about? How is that even possible?" I asked even more confused. "We don't even have the same last name."

"Dad had me before he was turned into a vampire. Before he even met your mother," Jonathan began to explain. I was so shocked I couldn't think of a single thing to say. "Say something. Aren't you excited? Not only are we business partners, but we are brothers too," Jonathan added as I continued to stare at him in shocked disbelief.

"Are we really brothers?" I asked him as though he hadn't just explained it all to me.

"We sure are!" Jonathan told me happily. "I have always gone by the last name Simmons, which was my mothers' maiden name. I didn't want any of the pressure that comes along with the Stallings name.

"That's awesome, man!" I always wanted a big brother!" I said. I wasn't sure how I felt about this sudden change of status between Jonathan and I. But, I knew he seemed super excited about it so I played along for now. I thought it was kind of weird it was just now coming out that we were brothers.

"So, what is the favor you wanted to ask me?" asked Jonathan.

"I was wondering if you had resources that might help us find Cameron," I told him.

"Who is Cameron?" Jonathan asked curiously.

"Cam is my elf." That was the best way I knew to put it. He was my elf, and I felt it was my responsibility to get him back.

"You have an elf?" Jonathan asked laughing.

"Yes I have an elf, and I need to save him." I began to tell Jonathan everything that had happened over the past week, starting with the abduction of Cam.

"Why didn't you come to me sooner? You know I am here for you anytime, bro," Jonathan explained.

I reminded him that I had been out of commission the whole week. I couldn't come see Jonathan being unconscious for a whole week. I began telling him everything we knew about the dark elf Devlin.

"Are you talking about the dark one?" Jonathan asked. I could tell his tone immediately changed to anger.

"Yes. Devlin is the one responsible for this. How do you know about him?" I asked curiously.

"The dark one stole the love of my life away from me several years ago. You need to be careful dealing with him. He is dangerous like you wouldn't believe. He took out a pack of my vampires all by himself. He killed Jessica for no good reason. Someone had hired him to get to me. His style is to take out the ones you love and force you to come to him," Jonathan explained.

"So that explains why he came after Ava with me standing right there. It also explains why he took Cam," I said as I began to put the pieces together.

"Luke, I want to help. Not just with Cam, but with everything. Dad stuck me here in Little Rock to look after this building, but after 60 years here, I am ready to move on," said Jonathan.

I suddenly had a flurry of ideas that I began to lay out in my head. "Why don't you come with me to England in the morning?" I asked. "I have a huge proposition for you," I told him. "Would you be interested in going to England to help run the family business?" I asked. If Jonathan was really my brother I wanted him to be happy and really be a part of the family.

"That sounds like a great idea. I will get my team on Devlin's trail and make arrangements here to be gone for a few days," Jonathan said excitedly.

"Why don't you meet me at the airport before dawn in the morning?" I asked.

"Sounds like a plan. I'll see you in the morning, bro," Jonathan said with a smile.

As soon as I made it back to my motorcycle in the parking lot I jumped in surprise when Jordan appeared right in front of me.

"He took Jack!" Jordan exclaimed.

"What do you mean? Who took Jack?" I asked confused.

"Devlin!" Jordan shouted.

"Jordan, calm down and tell me what happened," I said. I could tell she was very upset, but I needed her to settle down and tell me what was going on.

"Jack found where Devlin was hiding. He went in by himself trying to rescue Cam, but he never came back out," Jordan explained.

Jordan told me that Devlin had been hiding out in an abandoned building right there in downtown Little Rock. She gave me the address and I put it in my phone along with a quick message for Jonathan. He quickly responded telling me he would send a team to investigate.

I looked at Jordan and noticed she was crying. For the first time I realized Jordan was just like the rest of us soldiers. She was working day and night to protect us and find Cam. So what if she wanted to be a vampire. What would it hurt? In fact, the only thing I could think about was how her having the extra abilities would only help the soldiers. For a couple weeks I had been thinking about reasons not to turn her, but I couldn't come up with a single reason. I decided right then that I would have to learn how to turn somebody.

"You need to get some rest, Jordan. You have been tracking Devlin for a whole week now. There are lots of people on his trail now, and you could use a break. You look exhausted," I told her.

"But I don't want to stop until I find Cam and bring him back to you, Luke," Jordan said.

"I know you don't, but if you wear yourself completely out it want do anybody any good," I said.

I invited Jordan to come back and stay at the mansion for the night. There were plenty of extra rooms, and I knew she needed the rest.

"I already have plans for tonight," Jordan said.

"Why don't you meet me at the airport in the morning and you can come with us to England," I asked her.

"That sounds like a great idea!" Jordan said. I could tell she was happy I invited her to come along. "How about I just meet you tomorrow in England? Only takes me a quick second to be there," she laughed.

I knew she was right. Why would anybody want to endure a five hour flight when all they had to do was jump there in the blink of an eye? We said our goodbyes for the night and I headed back onto the highway toward Eerie.

The next morning I woke up early. I had set my alarm for four a.m. to give us plenty of time to make it to the airport before sunrise. When I got home the night before I had sent messages to everybody letting them know what time we were leaving. I was still really tired from the late night visit with Jonathan and was glad that I would be able to get more sleep on the flight.

I jumped in the shower and then quickly got dressed. I raced around and repacked the suitcase somebody had put away for me. I had everything together and headed out the door. By the time I made it downstairs, everybody was waiting for me. Ava, Dante, and Grandpa stood there looking just as tired as I was.

"Jonathan is going with us. I think I have a job for him to do in England," I told the group.

"Jonathan Simmons?" Grandpa asked. I was all too familiar with the gruff sound in Grandpa's voice when he wasn't too happy about something. "What business does he have in any of this?" I asked. I didn't understand why Grandpa would be upset other than the fact that Jonathan was a vampire.

I explained how Jonathan was my brother. I watched as Grandpa's face got redder and redder as I told them about everything.

"Jonathan cant be trusted, Luke. You need to be extra careful dealing with him," Grandpa said. "I trust you will always do the right thing, but I have to at least try to lead you down the right path."

"Jonathan has done nothing but help us for a couple years now," I said.

I suddenly realized I hadn't really ever told Grandpa anything about Jonathan and his coven. I continued to explain all of the things Jonathan had done to help me and the soldiers. "And he has his team looking into finding Cam," I added.

"Just be careful, Luke. That's all I'm saying. You don't want to be caught off guard if anything goes wrong. Vampires are only interested in things that will benefit them in the long run," Grandpa said.

"You must have forgotten that I am a vampire," I said sternly. "Is that what you think about me? And what about Dakota?" I asked as I began to get upset about what Grandpa was saying about vampires.

"Luke, please calm down. Your Grandpa is only looking out for you," said Ava.

For the first time since we met I suddenly was a little angry with Ava for taking Grandpa's side instead of mine. I felt a little betrayed, but I let it go. I knew they were only looking out for me, but I just wanted them to learn to trust my decisions.

"We better get going," said Dante. "Us VAMPIRES can't be out after the sun comes up," he added sarcastically.

When we got to the airport we all quickly boarded the plane. It was beginning to get light out, but the sun had not yet risen. Jonathan was waiting for us when we got there. Everyone settled in for the flight. I had planned to sleep, but Grandpa had gotten me so worked up about vampires that I was now wide awake.

Everyone else had fallen asleep when Lucy made a round to check on us. She asked if I needed anything and I asked her if Alexander kept any bottles of blood on the plane. I didn't even care anymore if anybody found out I was drinking it. Dakota made a good point about it being natural for me to want it. And I didn't really see anything wrong with it.

Lucy brought me a glass of the familiar thick red deliciousness. I was glad she didn't bring the whole bottle because I was afraid I would have put away the whole thing. I had a big day ahead of me and I needed to keep a clear head.

"Luke, there is something I need to tell you," said Ava. Her sudden voice startled me and I nearly spilled my glass all over myself.

"What's wrong, Ava?" I asked. I could tell that Ava had a concerned look on her face.

"Well, you know when I gave you that necklace," Ava started as she reached over and laid her had on my chest where the wolf's tooth hung. "I never told you the story behind it.

Ava began to tell me about this amazing wolf from many years ago that helped her grandfather in a great battle. The wolf was killed during the battle, and her grandfather, being a powerful wizard, used one of the wolf's teeth to make a powerful protection charm. She said she added the spell to hopefully increase its protection, and to make me stronger.

"Well, I think your creation has definitely served its purpose. It healed me for sure." I told her.

"That's the part I am concerned about. It was never meant to heal, only to protect," she said. "I think mixed with the blood you have been drinking it has evolved into something completely different."

"Why would you be concerned about me being healed and getting stronger? Isn't that what you created it for in the first place?" I asked.

"Luke, power changes people. I just don't want anything to happen to you is all," she said.

I felt as though there was more that she wasn't telling me, but I didn't press the issue. Great! One more thing I had to worry about. Like there wasn't already enough on my plate. What was up with this necklace? I asked myself as I slowly turned it around in my fingers studying it.

Suddenly my vision went black and I knew a vision was soon to follow. The vision came into focus. I instantly saw Nhados standing in the distance. What confused me about the whole situation was the fact that he was holding a newborn baby. Where did he get a baby from? I wondered. The scene flashed to Nhados again. But, this time instead of holding a baby, a young boy stood at his side smiling back at me.

I came to with Ava staring at me. She knew what had just happened. I told her about the vision and we both sat there thinking about what it could mean. Just another entry on the growing list of things I had to worry about. What's next? I asked myself.

Ava and I were quiet for the remainder of the flight. Neither of us could think of how a baby or a young boy played into what was going on in our lives. My visions always seemed to play themselves out no matter how good or bad. I guessed I would have to just wait and see what turned up. I finally drifted off to sleep. Just as I dozed off the plane touched down to the runway in England. So much for sleeping during the flight, I thought to myself.

Thomas was waiting on us when we touched down. We all piled into the hummer and headed for the castle. The main goal for this trip was to get all of my business in order so that I could go back to school without worrying about what was happening in England. The first order of business was to get the new Silent Soldiers England team up and operational. We had the whole day to work at the castle. Jonathan wouldn't be able to rise until after dark, and he played a part in the second half of my plan.

I was amazed as I watched out the window on the short journey to the castle. Grandpa had told me Eric and his team had been working to get the new headquarters established. I was shocked to see how much progress they had made. The airstrip and hangar were completely finished. The small dirt road leading to the castle was now a fully paved road.

Soon after leaving the runway, we came to a gate that hadn't been there the week before. I also noticed a fence running out from each side of the gate as far as I could see. My guess was that a new perimeter had been set up around the property. For some reason I suddenly thought back to the gnomes I had saved on our last trip. They had to feel safer being inside a locked area now. They shouldn't have to worry about any more ghouls attacking, or anything else for that matter.

"We probably should set up some protection spells around the perimeter like we have back at the mansion," I told Ava as we passed through the new security gate.

Ava smiled back at me and I knew she would be more than happy to show off her ever growing skills as one of the most powerful witches anyone had ever seen.

"I would be happy to," Ava said.

As I turned to look out the window again, I noticed Grandpa was also smiling at me. It was an amazing feeling knowing my family was proud of the things I was accomplishing.

When we got closer to the castle, I noticed the front entrance littered with trucks and vans from different companies. There was a security company, an electronics company, and several others. Another huge change I saw immediately was the giant satellite dish sitting on top of the castle. I became excited to see all of the progress Grandpa and Eric made while I was unconscious.

Thomas pulled the car through the front entrance and up to the front door. I quickly got out followed by Ava and

Grandpa. The sound of an electric motor drew my attention to the front door of the mansion. A small camera turned slowly until it was pointing directly at us. A few seconds later, Eric burst through the front doors grinning from ear to ear.

"Luke! You have no idea how happy I am to see you!" Eric exclaimed.

"Hey, Eric! It's great to see you again, buddy," I told him.

"I'm going to go freshen up while you boys catch up," Ava said giggling.

"You need some help with that?" I asked watching Ava struggle with her suitcase.

"Thanks, but I think I can handle it," said Ava smiling.

I watched as she continued to struggle a little bit. I switched to vampire mode and in the blink of an eye I grabbed the suitcase, deposited it on her bed in her room, and was back outside standing next to Eric smiling.

"Where did it go?" Ava asked confused. She looked up at me as I continued to smile at her.

"It's in your room, babe," I said. I winked at her and watched as she blushed a little. She walked over and pulled me down and put her lips to mine quickly.

"My hero! Have I told you how much I love you today?" Ava whispered.

This time I was the one to blush. "As a matter of fact, no, no you haven't," I replied.

Ava walked away into the castle leaving Eric to show Grandpa and I the progress that had been made. We followed him through the castle. He took us straight down toward the basement. My stomach suddenly turned to knots as I remembered my last trip down there. Once we made it to the end of the hall, I completely forgot about the bad experience with my father and became amazed by the things I was seeing.

The hall we went down led to a huge metal door with a familiar scan pad like the one back at the mansion.

"Try it out, Luke. The network is linked to the one at the castle, so you should be able to get in," said Eric.

I placed my hand on the pad and it began to scan. It told me access granted and the metal door slowly opened. We pushed our way in, and again I was amazed. I noticed several similarities to headquarters back at the mansion. There were several vehicles and motorcycles around the room, all black with our familiar logo. There was also a huge garage door at one end and I knew it was how the vehicles got in and out. We followed Eric over to one side where a man sat surrounded by t.v. screens and computer monitors. The man was so focused on the work he was doing I didn't thing he even notice we were standing there.

"The perimeter is clear. I just finished scanning the property," said the man. I guess he did know we were there after all.

"This is Sam. He is a networking genius. You can rest assured he has the control center covered," Eric said. "Sam, this is Luke. You already know Mr. Carrington."

"It's a pleasure to meet you Luke," Sam said as he stood up and extended his hand. "I am glad to see you are doing better. You were in pretty rough shape last time you were here."

"Thanks, it's nice to meet you too, Sam," I told him as I shook his hand.

Sam went back to work at the computers as Eric continued to show us around. I couldn't believe how much work they had done in only a week. It appeared as though the England headquarters was now fully operational.

"What do you think, Luke?" Eric asked. "The finishing touches with security and the network should be finished by this afternoon. We should be fully online and functional by morning."

"I think it is absolutely amazing how quickly you guys have put this place together!" I exclaimed. "I definitely made the right decision, and I am glad you and your pack agreed to stay here at the castle."

"Man, everybody loves all the extra room here. We didn't realize just how cramped we were back at the house," said Eric. "Thank you so much for inviting us."

"I couldn't think of a better team for the job," said Grandpa.

"I guess the only thing left to do is put together your team of soldiers," I told Eric. I didn't tell him I had a member in mind for him. My plans were to have Jordan join the England team.

"Well, I have actually been thinking about that. You, of course will have the final say, but I would like for me and my sister Katie to be members," said Eric excitedly.

"I would love to have you guys on board. There is a lot of training and preparation that goes along with being a soldier," I told him.

"We are ready, Luke. We are prepared to make the necessary sacrifices required to be a part of your amazing operation."

"It might be a good idea for you guys to come to the mansion. There are some amazing instructors there that have worked with me and my team for the past few years. What do you say?" I asked.

"That sounds great, buddy," said Eric. "I will make the necessary preparations. When should we come?"

"I will be here for a couple days. You are welcome to fly back with us if you are prepared to come that soon," I told him.

"We will be ready!" he exclaimed.

"What do you think Grandpa?" I asked as I looked over and saw him smiling back at me.

"I think it sounds like a great idea. It is exactly what I would do, Luke. I am so proud of you," Grandpa said.

"I have some things I need to take care of. Grandpa, can you work out travel and training details with Eric?" I asked.

"Of course I can, Luke. I am here for you any way I can help," said Grandpa.

I dismissed myself from the company of Eric and Grandpa. They had everything under control, and I had something I needed to discuss with Ava. I was happy to know Eric could handle things here at the castle. It was one thing I could mark off my list of things to worry about.

I used my super speed and was instantly outside the door to Ava's room knocking softly.

"Come in," I heard Ava say.

I opened the door and walked inside closing it behind me. Ava smiled at me as I made my way over to her. She was sitting on the bed and I climbed up beside her. I took her hand in mine and squeezed gently.

"Ava, there is something we need to talk about," I started.

"What's wrong?" Ava asked. I noticed the concern in her voice as I tried to find the words to proceed. I had no idea how Ava would take what I was about to tell her.

"Nothing is wrong. I just wanted to talk to you about Jordan. You know she has asked me several times to turn her. Well, I have actually been thinking about doing it," I told Ava. I waited nervously for her to respond.

"Why?" asked Ava. I was happy to notice that she didn't seem to be mad about the idea.

I began to explain to her about how much Jordan had helped us over the past couple weeks. I told her Jordan had been working day and night trying to find and rescue Cam. I tried to explain every detail that had led me to the decision I made about Jordan. I also told her how I thought her having vampire abilities would be great for the new Silent Soldiers team. I never expected the response I got after my explanation.

"Luke I think that sounds like a great idea. You know I trust you," she said.

"Wow, I never thought it would be that easy," I told her.

"I assure you the decision is not an easy one. But, you are the destined leader of the soldiers, Luke. I know that you would only do what you believe is best for us," Ava said as she smiled at me happily.

I couldn't believe Ava was ok with the decision I had made. I wasn't completely sure how I felt about it myself. I didn't know how the turning process even worked yet.

"Are you sure you're ok with me doing this?" I asked her.

"Of course I am. Why wouldn't I be? I mean she did save my life after all."

"What do you mean she saved your life? Did I miss something?" I asked confused. I wondered why Ava never told me anything about Jordan saving her.

"I thought I told you about when the dark elf attacked us," she said.

"I'm guessing you left out a few details."

"Well, after you hit the ground everything happened so fast I am still remembering little details myself," Ava said. "Once you were down, the elf jumped down between us. He grabbed Cameron and was just about to grab me when Jordan stepped in. She bear hugged the dark elf without thinking twice about it. Then they all three disappeared. If she hadn't saved me, I would be one of the dark ones hostages just like Cam." I noticed tears threatening to escape Ava's eyes. I squeezed her hand again gently to let her know I was here for her.

I was shocked by what Ava was telling me. I suddenly became very proud of Jordan for risking her life to save Ava from the clutches of the dark elf. I made a mental note to thank her for that the next time I saw her.

Once the sun went down Ava and I headed for the runway. Now that Jonathan had finally risen for the evening, we needed to go to my office. Grandpa said he had a few last minute details to work out with Eric. We left them to their tasks and shortly after were in the sky. I took the time during the flight to start telling Jonathan all about the current operations of Soldiers, Inc. That was the name Grandpa gave once he established the family business

Once we touched down at the airport and exited the plane I was surprised to see Thomas waiting there with the limo.

I was shocked to see him. I thought we had left him back at the castle. Seeing him standing here now, three hours from there, made me realize he wasn't human at all. It was funny, but it all started to make sense. Every time I needed Thomas, he was right there waiting with a car. I didn't even have to call and let him know.

Once we arrived at my building, Wendy greeted us as we walked in. "Good evening, Mr. Stallings. And welcome back, Mr. Simmons," she said smiling.

"Good evening, Wendy," Jonathan and I said at the same time. I guessed Jonathan had been here before. I wondered which of my deceased relatives he had visited. I guessed it had to be my father, since he and Jonathan were business partners.

"Been here before?" I asked Jonathan as we waited for the elevator to open.

"Yeah, man. I told you before that your father and I were partners," he replied.

"Good evening, Mr. Stallings, Mr. Simmons," Helen said as we entered my office. "Mr. Stallings, this just came for you," Helen said.

She handed me an envelope. I immediately noticed the fancy calligraphy style writing of my full name, Lucas Stallings, on the front of it.

"Thank you, Helen. Please hold all of our calls for a couple hours. We have a lot to discuss and we don't want to be interrupted, I told her. I wondered who would be sending me a letter, especially at the office.

Ava dismissed herself to go hang out in my apartment upstairs. I didn't blame her. I didn't want to be doing the business thing anymore than she did. But, it had to be done if I was ever going to have a life again. Grandpa and Jonathan followed me into my office and I heard the door close behind me.

"What's that letter you got there?" Jonathan asked.

"I don't know," I said as I looked down at it.

I turned the letter over and immediately recognized the seal on the back. It was the same seal that was tattooed on my chest. I glanced up to see Jonathan staring at the mysterious envelope. I wasn't positive, but I could almost swear Jonathan looked a little scared.

"Why don't you open it and see who it's from?" Grandpa asked.

I suddenly got knots in my stomach now that Grandpa's attention had been brought to the letter. My hands were shaking slightly as I carefully opened it. I sat down hard in the chair behind my desk after reading the letter's contents. I couldn't put into words how shocked I was about what I had just read.

"What does it say, Luke?" Grandpa asked. Jonathan remained silent as the fear registered on his face intensified.

I couldn't seem to make myself respond for several seconds. I was paralyzed in my seat.

137

"Luke, are you alright? What does it say?" Grandpa repeated.

"It says that I am to be named the leader of the England coven of vampires at midnight."

12

Everyone was quiet for some time as we thought about what we had just learned. I don't think anybody could think of a single thing to say being that we were shocked into silence.

"Why?" was the only word that I seemed to be able to say.

"I never thought they would pick you being so young," said Jonathan. He spoke so quietly I wondered if he even meant to say it out loud.

"You knew about this?" I asked.

"I knew they would appoint a new leader, but I never thought they would pick someone so young," Jonathan said.

"But I don't want to be the leader of the vampires. Why did they pick me?" I asked.

"Well, Luke, you are the next descendent of your grandfather, Alexander," said Grandpa. "It only makes sense for you to be next in line."

"There has to be a way around this!" I shouted.

"Luke, calm down buddy. The decision about being the leader lies with you. They want force you into the position. That being said, the decision shouldn't be made lightly. To be crowned the leader is a great honor," said Jonathan.

"Jonathan is right, Luke. You need to think about this before making a final decision," said Grandpa.

I looked at my watch and noticed it was only four hours until the expected coronation as the leader of the England vampires. Grandpa told me to think about it before I made a decision, but my mind was made up immediately. There was no way I was taking on another major responsibility. Not when I was working so hard to be able to go back to my normal life. I was determined I was going to take Ava to the homecoming dance one way or another. I explained to Jonathan and Grandpa how I felt about the situation we were in. I wasn't ready to become the adult my life was forcing me to be.

"You know if you accepted the position, you could choose anybody you wanted to fill in for you. You wouldn't have to be tied to it all the time," Jonathan explained.

"So, I can pick anybody I want?" I asked.

"Sure. The coven trusts their leader with everything they live for. All you have to do is pick somebody once you have accepted," said Jonathan.

"Fine, I pick you!" I told him excitedly.

The plan was perfect, I thought as I grinned from ear to ear at Jonathan. I had selected him to run my business in England. It only made sense that he lead the vampires too.

"Whoa, wait a minute! I didn't mean I wanted you to pick me," Jonathan said.

"Well, I guess I didn't think about it like that," I said. "Who else do we know that would want to take the position?"

"Hey, I didn't say I wasn't going to do it. I just want you to ask instead of just assuming I'm going to rescue you from the task. I'll only do it under one condition," Jonathan said.

"And what would that be?" I asked. I was willing to do just about anything to get out of being a vampire leader.

"You have to try and talk Mike Vance into taking over my spot in Little Rock," Jonathan said.

"Done!" I exclaimed. That would be a simple enough task to complete in order to get me back to my somewhat normal life back in Eerie.

"Well, now that is settled, can we get back to the task at hand?" Grandpa asked.

"I agree, Jonathan said."

I began explaining the role I wanted like Jonathan to play in my company. I explained that he would be in charge of day to day operations for the entire corporation. I wanted Jonathan to maintain the business at least until I got out of school. If I could just finish the last couple years of my childhood I would be happy. Jonathan agreed with everything I laid out for him. He even agreed with the part about getting all business decisions approved by Grandpa and me.

Once the business meeting of sorts was complete, it was nearly time for us to head off toward the coronation ceremony. My stomach was in knots to say the least. I had no clue what to expect from this meeting. I went up to the penthouse to quickly bring Ava up to speed about the change of plans for the evening and to grab my sword. I was about to break a rule I vowed to never break, and that was to never take non-vampires into the middle of a vampire coven. We met Grandpa and Jonathan in the lobby and headed outside where Thomas again met us with the car.

"So you are positive, if I accept this position, I can appoint anyone I want to stand in for me?" I asked again.

"I promise, Luke. I would never lie to my little brother," said Jonathan as he reached over and roughed up my hair.

We rode in silence for the remainder of the trip. I was surprised to realize we were heading deeper into downtown instead of out to some remote location. The car slowly pulled up to the curb in front of an office building about the size of the one Jonathan had back in Little Rock. We made our way through the front entrance and were greeted by a young vampire that couldn't have been much older than me. Well, he didn't appear to be much older. But, neither did Dakota, and he was over a hundred years old. The vampire didn't speak to us, but only motioned for us to follow him. As we followed the silent man onto the elevator I began to get the strange feeling I had only felt one other time. The same feeling I got when the dark one attacked us at the castle.

As the elevator went up, and we got closer to our destination, the nauseating feeling in my stomach got worse. The elevator stopped and we again followed the young vampire out into a room. The room contained a large table with chairs all around. Three other vampires rose from their seats as we entered the room. We watched as the young vampire walked around the table to take his place beside the other vamps.

"We want to welcome you, Mr. Stallings," said one of the vamps.

"Thanks," I replied as I looked around at the mostly empty room.

"Please have a seat," said another of the vamps motioning toward my group of my friends and family.

We all walked over and took a chair across from the vampires. They all smiled back at me curiously. The third vampire began to explain to me what being the head vampire entailed. Surprisingly he knew a lot about Alexander's business affairs. He began to tell me about a whole other set of businesses and properties my grandfather had owned that were now mine, including the building we were in. I looked over at Jonathan wondering if he knew what he was getting himself into. He noticed me looking and smiled back at me. He shook his head as though he know what I was thinking.

After the vampire concluded his speech about my grandfather and the England coven I realized Alexander had lived two separate lives. My grandfather was not only a very wealthy and powerful man in the human world, but he was also a very wealthy and fearless leader of this coven of vampires. The meeting definitely was not what I expected. I don't know exactly what I thought would happen, but I didn't expect a normal business meeting for sure.

The vampires went over each business and property. And, just like with the attorneys, I had documents to sign and sets of keys to collect. I had no idea what most of the businesses involved, but I wasn't going to worry about it. I trusted Jonathan to make sure everything was in order. This was the final piece in going back to my normal life and I was determined to not let anything mess up my plans. Once the vampires were through explaining everything, and all of the documents were signed, there was one final document.

"This is your acceptance as the leader of this coven, Mr. Stallings. We want to welcome you. If you ever need anything you can always contact us here anytime," one of the vampires said as I signed the final document.

"I am appointing Jonathan Simmons to look over the coven for a while. All contact should go through him regarding the business we just discussed," I told them not wasting any time.

"That can be arranged," said one of the vamps. "We will have the documents drawn up and you can come by first thing in the morning to sign them."

I looked over and noticed Ava yawning next to me. It was into the wee hours of the morning and I was pretty tired myself. I ended the meeting and we all headed back to my condo for the night. I wanted to go to the castle tonight and finalize all of the preparations and then fly home, but now we had to wait around to sign more documents.

I woke up earlier than I expected. I had only been asleep for a short time, but I felt rested enough to start the day. I grabbed my cell phone and noticed there was a message that said the documents are ready. It said I could stop by any time to sign them. I quickly got dressed for the day and left a note on the counter. Everyone was still sleeping so I decided to get the signing out of the way while I waited for them to wake up. I was more than ready to get everything done so we could go back to the mansion. If I could make it back to school by tomorrow, I would have a few days of practice to get ready for the homecoming game.

When I arrived back in the building from the previous night, I noticed something I hadn't noticed the night before. With the sun being out I was surprised to find out the windows were completely blacked out. The only light in the lobby was that from a small lamp sitting on a desk inside the door despite the whole front of the building being windows. Once again the strange feeling came over me. The young vampire from the night before sat at the desk. I wondered why he hadn't retired for the evening like other vampires.

The boy motioned for me to follow him as he headed toward the elevator again without speaking. I followed him in and the doors closed behind us. As soon as the doors closed the young vamp spoke for the first time.

"You need to be careful dealing with Jonathan Simmons," the vamp said with a heavy unfamiliar accent.

"Why?" I asked him immediately taking a defensive tone.

"Mr. Simmons cannot be trusted," was all he said.

"Well I think I can make that decision for myself," I told him.

The vamp didn't speak again he only nodded his head in agreement. Jonathan had never done anything to make me question his loyalty. Unless this guy could give me a good reason not to trust Jonathan, he would continue to be the one I didn't trust. I wondered why he didn't elaborate on the horrible statement he made about somebody I considered to be family.

The doors to the elevator opened before I could ask him any questions. The same large room from the night before came into view. The only difference was there weren't any vampires waiting for us when we exited the elevator.

"Where are they?" I asked.

"They are asleep for the day. The documents you need to sign are right here," he said as he motioned toward a small stack of papers lying on the table.

"Where do I sign?" I asked him.

"Are you sure you know what you're doing?"

"Why don't you quit playing games and just tell me whatever it is you keep insinuating," I said bluntly.

"I don't believe you know Mr. Simmons as well as you think," he responded.

"What does that even mean? Are you going to tell me what it is you think you know about Jonathan?

"I know lots, Mr. Stallings. I have been around for many centuries," The vamp said. Why don't you ask Jonathan about his past?"" said the vamp.

I suddenly realized the vampire definitely wasn't as young as he looked. I wondered briefly about the things he had been through and seen in all the years he had been alive.

"I just want to sign the papers and get back to my life. I only have a couple years to be a kid and I want them to be as normal as possible," I said.

"I'm not telling you not to sign the papers, Lucas. That decision is yours completely. I am only warning you to be careful," the vamp explained.

I was so confused. He kept telling me I couldn't trust Jonathan. Now he was telling me it was my decision to sign. He was right about me knowing nothing about Jonathan's past. But, he had been nothing but good to me since I met him. I had to at least give Jonathan a chance. Until he proved he couldn't be trusted I was ok with proceeding with my original plans.

"I don't even know your name, Dude!" I said to the vampire.

"My friends call me Demi," he replied.

"Well, Demi, I think I want to just sign the papers for now. Jonathan is my friend and I trust him. At least until somebody can prove otherwise," I said sarcastically.

"Very well, Mr. Stallings," Demi said as he handed me a pen and showed me where to sign.

He gave me a copy of the document I had just signed and I made my exit. As soon as I got in the car my ringtone sounded and I dug it out of my pocket to check my phone. It was a message from Matt.

"Dude, when are you coming home?" I need you buddy! We got a new coach and he really sucks. You don't want to miss the big game Friday night!" I read.

"Wrapping things up, hope to be back by morning!" I sent him in response.

With the final order of business in place I was just about ready to go home. Checking on Eric and his crew at the castle was the only other thing I needed to do. As the car made its way back to my building I wondered what was going on back home. Why did we have a new coach? It seemed as though the normal life I was trying to get back to wasn't quite as normal as I wanted it to be.

Grandpa and Ava were awake when I got back to the condo. I walked straight up to Ava and gave her a kiss.

"What was that for?" She asked smiling up at me after I finally let her go.

"I'm just happy!" I exclaimed. "I'm ready to go home as soon as we finish at the castle. I'm happy we can finally get back to our lives."

"Actually, Luke, everything at the castle is complete. The last of the construction crews left yesterday afternoon. I just got off the phone with Eric. He and Katie will be at the mansion by the weekend to begin their training," Grandpa said.

"That's great news. I'll call Grady and let him know to have the plane ready," I said.

I didn't wait for any response from Ava or Grandpa. I immediately grabbed my phone and made the call. In less than an hour we were on a plane headed for Little Rock. We were finally on our way home.

"Welcome back guys!" Matt yelled as we walked down the steps of my plane.

"Man, you have no idea how happy we are to be back," I said.

"We want to hear every detail," said Jenna.

"I don't really know where to start. It's been a busy week," I said once we were in the car headed toward the mansion.

I tried to explain everything that happened in England in as much detail as possible. I knew Matt and Jenna hated they weren't able to go with us. They didn't know how much I would have rather been at school with them.

"So you're like a vampire king now?" Matt asked once I finished my story. "Dude, that is so cool!"

"I'm not a king, Matt," I said even though technically I guess I really was.

"Whatever, man. We are just glad you are finally home," Matt replied.

"Your mom is going to be so happy to see you. She was worried you weren't going to make it back to the wedding Saturday," said Jenna.

"I would never miss my mom's wedding," I lied. I had completely forgotten about the wedding all together. I was so focused on the big game and the dance. I felt horrible about forgetting something so important to mom.

The rest of the evening was uneventful. Matt and Jenna helped Ava and I get caught up on all of our homework. I retired to my room early. I was exhausted from all the excitement the past few days. I just wanted to crawl into my bed that I had missed so much. I fell asleep almost immediately.

The next morning I woke up before the alarm even went off. I got up and showered and got dressed and was excited like it was the first day of school. I met Ava, Matt, and Jenna in the dining hall for breakfast and we headed to school.

"So, you never told me why we have a new coach. What happened to our old one?" I asked.

"I don't know man. Yesterday when I went to gym class this new guy was there. He said he would be coaching for the rest of the year. He never said why," Matt explained.

"That seems kind of weird that coach would leave in the middle of the season like that," I said.

The day went by pretty fast and it was finally time for gym. As soon as I walked into the gym the strange feeling I had been having returned. I couldn't seem to put my finger on what was causing the strange feeling. I had never felt anything like it, so I had nothing to compare it to.

I spotted the new coach standing next to the locker room door. He was standing there with his arms crossed looking like a prison guard keeping watch over his subjects. Our eyes suddenly met and I watched as the corners of his mouth turned up into a half grin.

"You must be Luke, I presume," said the coach as I made it to the locker room door to change clothes for class.

"Yes, I'm Luke," I replied.

"I hear you have some arm on you, kid," said the coach as a huge grin spread across his face.

He reached out his hand to shake. I took it and was surprised that he held on to it a lot longer than I would have thought was necessary.

"Can I have my hand back?" I asked him.

"Oh, sorry about that," said coach. "I can't wait to see if all the rumors I hear about you are true."

The rest of the day went by just as quickly as the first part. We all talked excitedly as we made our way home. The next day was the big day and we were all anticipating the festivities.

The football team surprised me that night. They played better than ever. Matt and I didn't even have to use any of our abilities to completely blow out the team we were playing. They didn't even come close to scoring a single point the whole game.

It was almost disappointing not having any competition. After the game we hurried to the locker room to get ready for the second and most important half of the evening. I was super excited about taking my beautiful date to the homecoming dance.

As we come out of the field house our night suddenly took a turn for the worse. Suddenly Jordan appeared right in front of us clutching a small unconscious elf in each of her hands.

"I did it!" Jordan said. I watched in horror as the three of them crumpled to the ground.

"Jordan!" I yelled as I saw the familiar arrow sticking out of her back. Jordan had been shot by the dark elf with one of the same arrows he used to shoot me.

13

"Call Grandpa!" I yelled at Matt before I noticed he already had his phone out dialing.

Once I felt Jordan, Jack, and Cam all had fairly strong pulses I quickly sent Ava a message letting them know where we were.

Within a couple minutes Ava and Jenna came running up to us. I stopped what I was doing immediately when I realized how beautiful Ava was. The black dress she was wearing looked amazing as it clung to the curves of her body perfectly. Even in near darkness I could see her hair pulled loosely to the top of her head revealing her amazing neckline. I could see the veins in her neck pulsing in time with the beat of her heart. The only thing that pulled my eyes from her beauty was the sudden return of the strange feeling in the center of my chest. The sick feeling in my stomach wasn't far behind.

"You took something from me," I heard a voice hiss from behind me. "You must pay with your lives,"

I quickly turned to the sound of the voice and was horrified as I stared at the dark elf pulling an arrow into his bow. Suddenly blue bolts of electricity shot from behind me toward the elf knocking him backwards through the air several feet. The electricity was followed closely by the familiar puff of purple smoke from one of Ava's capture spells. When the smoke finally cleared we all stared in shock. The familiar silver net from the spell lay on the ground empty.

"What just happened?" Matt asked.

Everything had happened so fast that Matt hadn't seen anything with his back to us while on the phone with Grandpa.

"It was the dark elf," I told him.

"Where did he go?" Jenna asked looking around anxiously.

"I don't know. How did he escape my spell?" asked Ava.

"Elves are not affected by silver," said Cam.

We all looked down and noticed he had come to and was raised up on one elbow. I quickly went over and helped him up off the ground.

"Are you ok, buddy?" I asked my friend Cam.

"I'll be fine. The dark one put some kind of spell on us, but I think it is wearing off now," he told us.

About that time Jack started to stir as well. Ava helped Jack to his feet as three black vehicles sped up to our location. I noticed immediately it was Grandpa and several of the other pack members.

"Jack, Cam, can you take Jordan to the mansion? I'll call Dr. Blevins and have her meet you," I said.

In an instant the three of them disappeared as I pulled out my cell phone to call the doctor. She told me that she was already at the mansion on other business and was ready as soon as they arrived.

"What happened here?" I heard Grandpa say to Matt, Ava, and Jenna as I made my way over to them.

"Jordan rescued Cam and Jack. The dark elf followed her here to get them back, but Ava and Jenna intervened," Matt explained.

"Where is he now? Grandpa asked.

"We don't know. I threw a capture spell at him but he escaped somehow," Ava said.

I could tell she was a little upset that her spell hadn't worked. I walked over and hugged her trying to show her that it was ok. She smiled up at me, but I could tell she was mad about it.

"You guys should go enjoy the dance," I said to Matt, Jenna, and Ava. "There really isn't anything else we can do. She is in the hands of Dr. Blevins now."

"Are you sure?" asked Matt and Jenna at the same time.

"I'm positive. Go have fun. I'll see you guys when you get home," I said.

"I'm not going without you, Luke," said Ava.

"I'm sorry," I told her.

"Sorry for what?" she asked.

"I'm sorry you are missing the dance," I said.

"Luke, it's not your fault," said Ava.

"I know, I just wanted us to have a normal night. I didn't want anything like this to ruin it for you," I said.

"Luke, just being with you makes any night a great one!" Ava said causing me to blush.

The thought of the arrow sticking out of Jordan's back flashed into my head. I realized I needed to get back to the mansion to check on her.

"We need to get home. I have to check on Jordan. The elf shot her with an arrow," I told Grandpa.

"Let's go!" Grandpa responded in a very serious tone.

I noticed the expression of fear spread across his face and knew he was worried. Would Jordan be able to fight off the effects of the poison from the arrow? I thought to myself. Was she strong enough to pull through? Matt and Jenna headed toward the dance while Ava and I raced toward my car to go home. I made it there in record time, several minutes before Grandpa and the rest of the pack.

When we made it to headquarters Dr. Blevins was already tending to Jordan's wounds. She was working to get the arrow out of her back. Jack and Cameron sat against one wall watching Jordan being cared for. They both owed her their lives for saving them from the dark one.

"How is she?" I asked fearing the worst.

"It is still too early to tell, but it doesn't look good. Her body isn't nearly as strong as yours, Luke," Dr. Blevins told us.

We watched as the doctor finished removing the arrow and sewed the wound closed.

"Is there anything we can do to help?" I asked.

"I'm afraid not, Luke. She must fight off the poison if she is going to survive," said Dr. Blevins.

Dr. Blevins adjusted the medication going into Jordan's arm before dismissing herself from the room.

"I know what I have to do to save her," I told Ava once we were alone with Jordan.

"Do you think that will save her?" asked Ava.

"I think it is our only option at this point. I refuse to stand here and let her die. It's what she would want me to do. She has been begging me for weeks," I explained trying to rationalize what I was about to do.

"I agree. It is definitely worth a shot. But, do you even know how?" Ava asked.

"I think so. I have been studying about it. Jonathan even explained it to me. It seems like a fairly easy process," I said.

"If you can save her you should definitely try," said Cam from where he and Jack sat in the room. "She saved us!"

Suddenly the heart machine that had been beeping steadily went wild with all kinds of alarms sounding. Dr. Blevins burst through the doors.

"We're losing her," said Dr. Blevins as she began to perform chest compressions to keep her heart beating.

"It's now or never, Luke," Ava said.

I rushed to Jordan's side and turned her head to expose the huge vein in her neck. Without even thinking I sank my fangs deep into the vein. The taste that flooded my senses was unlike anything I had ever tasted. It tasted so much better than the bottled stuff Alexander had created. I felt a sudden surge of power that I had never felt in all my life.

"Luke!" I heard Ava shout from beside me. I guessed I had drank a little longer than Ava thought I should have.

"What are you doing?" shouted Dr. Blevins as I released my bite from Jordan's neck and sank my fangs into my own wrist.

I held my wrist on Jordan's mouth allowing the flow of blood to run in and down her throat. From what I read, and what Jonathan told me, I had to consume the persons' blood and then feed them my own. As far as I knew I had completed the task of turning Jordan into a vampire.

The sound of the steady beep indicating Jordan's heart had stopped beating was deafening.

"What have you done?" I heard Grandpa say after he burst into the room.

"I couldn't let her die!" I shouted.

"It was the only way to save her life," Dr. Blevins said. "She surely would have died."

"Did it work?" asked Ava.

"I guess we will find out in twenty-four hours. Jonathan said that's how long the transformation takes," I said.

"I'll stay with her," said Dr. Blevins as she began to disconnect Jordan from all the machines.

"Luke, you can't just go around turning people," Grandpa said.

"She begged me to turn her for weeks. If I had done it sooner maybe she wouldn't be in this shape right now," I told him.

"Why didn't you tell me?" asked Grandpa.

I knew the reason I hadn't told him was because I knew he would react just like he was now. I remained silent as he continued to stare at me waiting for an answer.

"I don't know Grandpa. I just didn't want you to be upset with me about it," I told him.

"You two should get some rest. Tomorrow is a big day for your mother and Dante," Grandpa said.

Ava and I took this as our cue to leave. I didn't want Grandpa lecturing me anymore about turning Jordan. I just hoped the process worked. I really wanted to question Jack and Cam about their imprisonment with the dark one, but I guessed it would have to wait until later.

I kissed Ava good night when we made it to her door.

"I'm proud of you for trying to save her life, Luke."

"Thanks," I said.

Her statement actually made me feel a little bit better about the whole situation. I kissed her again and headed for my room. I didn't know if I could go to sleep or not, but I was tired to say the least. I crawled into bed and was asleep before I knew it. The dream was the same as before. Nhados standing there smiling holding a newborn baby. The scene then flashed to the young boy standing at Nhados' side both smiling at me eerily.

Despite the dream I woke up feeling rested the next morning. Mom and Dante's wedding wasn't until later in the evening. I showered and got dressed and grabbed my laptop. Dante and his team had added security camera feeds to the hospital wing as well as the holding cells. I quickly logged into the network to check on Jordan. I was surprised to find her sitting up on the side of the bed. I jumped off the bed as fast as I could and raced through the mansion in a blur. I was at Jordan's side within seconds.

"Jordan! You're ok!" I exclaimed.

Jordan jumped and tried to get away as if someone was trying to attack her.

"Luke! You scared the crap out of me!" Jordan said.

"I'm sorry," I told her as I slowly walked over to sit down on the bed.

"What has happened to me?" she asked.

"You almost died," I said. "I turned you just as your heart stopped beating."

"Really?" she asked curiously.

I watched as she stood up and walked across the floor. She had on a hospital gown and held it together in the back to hide her butt. I immediately noticed the wound from the arrow in her back was completely gone.

"How long have I been out?" she asked.

"Not nearly as long as I thought you would be. I thought it was supposed to take twenty-four hours for somebody to turn," I said confused.

Suddenly Jordan ran over to me and threw her arms around my neck.

"You saved me!" Jordan exclaimed. "Thank you so much, Luke!"

"I couldn't let you die, Jordan. I had to do something, and it was what you wanted, right?" I asked.

"Of course it is! I am so happy. Thank you thank you thank you," Jordan kept repeating.

Just then I heard the door open behind us. Jordan released me from her grip. I would have to remind her she was stronger than she realized. I turned to see that Ava had entered the room.

"Jordan! How are you awake so fast?" Ava asked.

"I don't really know," said Jordan.

"I'm just glad you're ok," I said.

"You did it, Luke. You saved Jordan's life," said Ava.

Suddenly there was a familiar pop sound and we all stared at Patrick now standing right in front of us.

"What are you doing here Patrick?" Jordan asked.

"How did you get in here? We have protection spells up to keep people from popping in," said Ava.

"I had to make sure my little sis was ok,' said Patrick smiling.

"Jordan is your sister?" I asked.

"Actually, I am his half-sister. We had different fathers," Jordan explained.

"I hear you are recruiting for a new team of soldiers," Patrick said. "I want in."

"Who told you that?" Ava asked.

I didn't know it was public knowledge about the new England team. It made me curious that maybe Patrick had been spying on us, especially since he could just pop in at the soldiers headquarters.

"Hey I didn't mean to step on anybody's toes. I just want to help," said Patrick.

I suddenly thought about how Patrick had only ever tried to help us in the past. We hadn't seen any sign of him since we captured all of his brothers and sisters that worked for Thados.

"We can use all the help we can get against this dark elf," I said.

"I guess you are right about that, Luke," said Ava.

"Well, I was actually going to talk to Jordan about joining. It would be great to have you both on board," I said. "You would have to complete the training program with Eric and Katie. Eric is in charge of the England team. When they arrive this weekend we can talk to them about it," I explained.

"Mom is worried about you, Jordan. You should go see her," said Patrick.

"Ok, we can go right now. You just have to let me get dressed first," said Jordan.

"I brought you some clothes to wear. The ones you have on are covered in blood," said Ava. We all noticed the clothes she was holding for the first time.

Ava handed the clothes to Jordan. Jordan was a blur for a fraction of a second and then she stood in front of us fully dressed.

"I guess you have your speed all figured out," I told Jordan.

"Let's go, Patrick, before Mom decides to come looking for me," said Jordan. "Wait, I don't know if I still have my elf powers," she added.

"Try it," said Patrick.

Jordan suddenly vanished right before our eyes. I looked at Patrick and he smiled. Jordan had confirmed she was still equipped with her elf powers.

"I will call you when Eric and Katie arrive so we can talk about your training," I told Patrick.

I watched as Patrick nodded in agreement before he too vanished. I looked over to Ava and she shrugged her shoulders indicating she was just as confused as I was about what just happened. Jordan had made a miraculous transformation in a fraction of the normal time it takes to turn into a vampire. Patrick showed up out of nowhere and we found out he was Jordan's brother and offered to join the soldiers. And that was all before breakfast. What else would this day bring?

Ava and I spent the day together. We walked around the mansion hand in hand watching as caterers and decorators furiously prepared for my mom's wedding. Everything was turning out to be so beautiful. I thought to myself how much my mother deserved this day. Her whole marriage to my father had pretty much been a joke. At least now she had met someone I believed would lay down his life for her. He would take good care of her. If he didn't, he would have me and the rest of the pack to deal with.

Ava and I stood with the rest of the guests as the preacher welcomed them and announced the wedding was to begin. I noticed the look of pride on Dante's face as he made his way down the aisle. When he passed me he purposely made eye contact and a huge smile spread across his face. I couldn't help but smile back at him. I was happy he was joining our family.

Once Dante made it to the alter the music changed announcing the coming entrance of Mom. Everyone stood and turned toward where she would come out. When she stepped out into the setting sun I couldn't believe how beautiful she was. I stared in awe as Grandpa escorted her slowly down the aisle to meet Dante at the alter. Grandpa gave the hand he was holding to Dante. He smiled and took mom's hand eagerly. They both turned toward the elderly man that was to walk the bride and groom through their vows to become husband and wife.

Suddenly the strange feeling I had been experiencing lately returned in full force. I thought I might even throw up it got so strong and made me sick to my stomach. I began looking around for a possible source. From past experiences my instincts told me there was danger lurking.

"What's wrong, Luke?" asked Ava from beside me.

"I'm not sure. Something doesn't feel right," I told her as I continued to scan the area as quickly as possible.

In a flash I ran to my room and grabbed my sword. Before Ava knew what was happening, I was back beside her, holding it.

"Luke! What are you doing?" Ava asked as she began to nervously look around the crowd herself.

Just then there was a sudden gasp from several of the guests. I noticed quickly found out what they were looking and I was instantly horrified by it. Standing behind Dante and my mother was the dark one. He stared right at me and smiled. I was frozen in place with fear.

"Two for two," hissed the dark one.

I willed my body to move as I pulled the sword from its sheath which caused me to transform instantly to the white outfit. I started forward with the sword held high. I was prepared to cut this elf in half if only I could get to him in time. Just before I reached the alter, to bring the sword down on top of his head, he quickly turned and grabbed Dante and my mother by the arm and disappeared.

My sword sliced right through the platform where the dark elf had just stood. I fell to my knees as an uncontrollable scream of anger escaped my mouth. We had finally got Cam and Jack back, and now we were in the same predicament. The dark one had disappeared taking my parents with him.

14

I couldn't seem to control the anger that seemed to be taking over my body. I continued to scream out several more times before I felt Ava put her hand on my shoulder. I knew it was her because I could smell her perfume before she even reached my side. My senses were in overdrive as my mind raced trying to figure out how to get them back.

"Luke, please calm down. You are scaring me a little bit," said Ava.

The sound of her voice seemed to calm me somewhat. At least enough that I could finally control my own movements. I was finally able to stop yelling out.

"He took her!" I shouted at her. "Don't tell me to calm down!" I said, immediately regretting how the words came out. I realized that I had truly hurt Ava for the first time. I saw tears well up in her eyes. "I'm sorry, Ava."

I knew shouting and being mean to the people that wanted to help wasn't going to get my mother and Dante back. I felt horrible and hoped Ava would understand how sorry I really was.

"Luke, I know a terrible thing just happened, but screaming and being ugly to people is not going to get them back," Ava said as if she read my mind. "Now, what can we do?" she asked.

"Luke, are you alright?" Grandpa asked as he bent down to help me back to my feet.

"No! I am definitely not ok!" I shouted.

"I'm sorry, Luke. I promise you I will do everything in my power to get them back," growled Grandpa.

He walked away briskly pulling out his phone. I continued to hear him growl orders into his phone.

"I want the leaders of every pack here NOW!" I heard Grandpa shout.

I felt sorry for snapping at Grandpa. But I realized he would do absolutely anything to get his daughter back. My mind began to spin again as I tried to think of anything the soldiers could do to find my mother.

"We should get everybody together, Luke. Maybe we can come up with an idea as a team," said Ava.

"That's a great idea. Let's go now," I said.

I quickly pulled out my cell phone and sent a message for everyone to meet us at headquarters. The sun had set for the evening so I knew Dakota would be able to come as well. By the time everyone arrived, I had calmed down quite a bit. I was still upset about my mom being taken, but I knew I needed a level head if we were to come up with a way to get them back.

"Thanks for coming, guys," I said to the group once everybody was there.

"We are so sorry to hear about your parents," Dakota said motioning to me and Jenna.

I couldn't believe I had been so selfish that I hadn't even thought about the fact that Jenna's dad had been taken too. I could see that she had been crying.

"The reason I called you all here is to come up with something we can do to try and get them back," I told them.

I watched as Jenna got up and walked over to a computer someone had left on the conference table. She placed both hands over the keyboard and closed her eyes as everyone watched and waited for her to find something.

"Nobody has seen the dark one," Jenna said. "There is not one single thing anywhere about the elf being spotted at all," said Jenna.

I noticed the disappointment in her tone and smelled her tears even before they began to run down her cheeks. At that moment I felt closer to Jenna than ever before. Both our parents being taken definitely seemed to bring us closer together.

"What about Jordan?" asked Ava.

"Who is Jordan?" asked Matt.

I remembered that Ava and I hadn't really talked to any of the other soldiers lately. I began to explain to them how Jordan had been one of the green eyed vamps. I told them everything we had been through over the past couple of weeks. I watched as all of their mouths dropped open with the news that I had turned her to save her life.

"You turned somebody into a vampire?" Matt asked. "That is so cool!"

Jenna slapped Matt on the arm and gave him an evil stare. He just looked at her confused, not knowing why he had been hit.

I went on to quickly bring the group up to speed on the new Silent Soldiers England team before I pulled out my phone and sent a message to Jordan. Jordan appeared before I could even put my phone back in my pocket.

"Hey guys," she said cheerfully. "What's wrong?" she asked once she realized none of us were smiling back at her.

"We need to know how you found the dark one," I told her after I explained how my mom and Dante had just been taken.

"Oh no!" Jordan exclaimed.

"Do you think you can help? You are the only one that has been able to find him so far," I said.

"I don't know if I can find him again," said Jordan.

"What do you mean? You found him before," said Ava.

"I know, but I only got lucky. I kept jumping to several different locations where I heard he had been spotted. I jumped back and forth and he actually showed up," explained Jordan.

"He will be much harder to find this time. I'm sure he didn't take too kindly having his hostages stolen away from him before," said Dakota.

"I guess you're right," I said sadly.

"Luke, you know we are going to do what we can to find you guys parents," Matt said.

"I know you will, and Grandpa has every werewolf in the country looking for them too. There is something else I wanted to talk to you all about," I told them.

"What's up?" asked Matt.

I told them about the strange feelings I had been having. I told them the first time was when the dark one attacked. Next was when I met Demi in England, which led into the whole story about being the leader of the England coven. Lastly, I told them about having the feeling around the new coach at school.

"What do you think it means?" asked Jenna.

"I don't know. That's why I am telling you about it so you might help me figure it out," I said.

"Well, do they have anything in common?" asked Matt.

"Not that I know of, one is an elf, one is a vampire, and one is human," I replied.

"Maybe we should keep an eye on the coach and see if we can figure anything out," said Ava.

"That is probably a good idea," said Dakota.

"Thanks for coming, Jordan. Eric and Katie should be here tomorrow to go over the training schedule. Are you and Patrick still planning on coming?" I asked.

"Of course!" exclaimed Jordan.

Jordan dismissed herself to go back to the business I had pulled her away from. Just as she disappeared I wondered to myself why she wasn't asleep. Vampires slept during the day, but Jordan definitely didn't seem to be a normal vampire.

We left the conference room headed our own separate directions. Ava stayed with me and I was glad. I didn't want to be by myself. I knew I needed something to keep my mind off the problems at hand. We headed toward Grandpa's office to see what he had found out so far.

"Your Grandpa just left to go and see the elders at the council. He is demanding the do something to help find your mother and Dante," said Grandma once we made it to Grandpa's office.

I became even angrier about the whole situation. I knew everybody was doing what they could, but I felt like I was doing nothing at all. I should be out looking for them, but where would I even start? The only thing I could do was stay calm and hope someone would spot the dark one. Then we would be able to attack and get our parents back.

The next day all of the members from the England team of soldiers arrived. I showed them to their rooms first. Next, I took them to meet the trainers and instructors they would be working with for the next few weeks. They all were very excited about becoming the newest members of the team. I was excited for them, but I know I didn't show it because I was still way too worried about Mom.

The rest of the day was uneventful. We searched all day for any possible dark elf sightings with no results. Grandpa arrived late in the evening from his meeting with the council. I couldn't wait to hear what they had to say.

"Luke, they really can't do any more than is already being done. They have teams all over the world looking out for the dark one to appear. They will contact us if they hear any news," Grandpa explained.

This was not what I wanted to hear. I wanted to hear that search parties were scanning the globe in search of my mother and Dante. I knew there was nothing anybody could do until the dark one was spotted.

The next morning we decided to go to school. One reason was to keep me busy as I waited around to hear something about my mother. The second reason was the new coach needed to be watched in order to figure out why he caused me to have the strange feelings. It was driving me crazy not being able to rush to my mother's side to try and save her. I needed to focus my attention on something other than that.

We took shifts between classes watching the coach. At lunch we talked about how boring it was following a normal teacher. Everything about him told us he was just a normal football coach, except for my strange feelings. Once we finished football practice in gym class I was questioning these new feelings all together. If I didn't know any better I would say our old coach acted stranger than the new one.

That afternoon after school the soldiers gathered in my room to discuss the coach.

"Why don't we try to search the internet and see what we can find out about the coach," I said.

We watched as Jenna went into the computer and began searching.

"I found him!" Jenna exclaimed. His name is James Doyle. He is fifty-three years old, and he was born and raised in Chicago. I don't see that he has ever been married," Jenna said.

We all moved to look at the screen to see the picture Jenna had brought up showing James Doyle, our new coach, as a teenager in a United States Army uniform.

"He was in the army?" Matt asked.

"That's what it says," said Jenna.

"Are we sure we should be worried about a U.S. veteran?" asked Matt.

"If Luke thinks we need to watch the coach then we should watch him," said Ava defending me.

"I'm only telling you guys he is one of the few things that has caused the strange feelings. If you don't want to keep an eye on him I can do it myself," I said.

"We didn't say we weren't going to help, man!" said Matt.

"We are just trying to figure this out, Luke. I mean, he seems like an ordinary old guy," said Jenna.

"Why are you so touchy lately?" asked Matt. "You should know by now that we are behind you a hundred percent, buddy."

"I'm sorry guys, just really stressed right now. I think I need to go for a run to unwind a bit. Anybody want to join me?" I asked trying to lighten the mood.

The tension was so thick in the room I could have sliced through it with my sword. I didn't have to wait long before everyone agreed with my idea. It had been a while since I had even shifted into a wolf at all. I was suddenly very excited about it.

I looked at Ava once I remembered every time I suggested running I was leaving her out.

"We could do something else," I told her.

"No, you guys go ahead. I have some things I need to do. I could go if I wanted," she said smiling.

I had forgotten all about Ava making a potion that let her shift. I wished she wanted to go, but I was going no matter what. There was something I needed to do, and I needed some free time.

The three of us nearly broke into a run as we made our way downstairs and to the garden at the back of the mansion. I shifted before I even made it out the doors. I couldn't wait. I didn't waste any time taking care of the task I had in mind. I couldn't believe I hadn't thought about it sooner.

I noticed the decorations from the wedding had already been taken down. All of the chairs, however, were still in place. I made my way up the aisle to the platform where I last saw my mom. Remembering this definitely didn't help in the stress department. I shook the thoughts from my mind as I arrived at my destination. I looked down and my eyes were drawn to the two separate sections where my sword had sliced through easily.

I put my nose down to the wood and started analyzing the different smells coming from it. I quickly picked up the familiar scent of my mom and Dante. I lingered at the scent of my mother before continuing my search. Suddenly I found what I was looking for. I had found the scent left by the creature I was hunting. I locked onto it. I wanted the scent burned into my brain so I would never forget it. A quiet growl escaped from my throat as I continued to inhale.

"Luke! What's wrong, man?" I heard Matt say in my head.

"Just trying to remember the smell of that stupid elf that took Mom," I thought back to him.

I watched as Matt and Jenna both walked over and sniffed the platform. I heard Jenna growl and knew she probably felt the same way I did.

"Got it!" said Matt's voice inside my head.

Now that I had finished my task I was ready for the main reason for the adventure in the first place.

"Let's go!" I heard Matt say.

I watched as Matt and Jenna broke into a full run. I watched for several seconds as they disappeared into the forest. I gave them a few more seconds before taking off at vampire speed. I slowed down once I caught up with Matt and Jenna. We were finally free for our very long deserved run. I let out a howl as we continued to run full speed ahead.

15

The next day at school we continued our surveillance of the coach, or James Doyle, or whoever he was. We decided he was never going to do anything unnatural at school and risk being exposed. That led us to our next idea to follow him after school. When class was over for the day we waited around in the parking lot. We ended up having to move once we were one of only two cars left. We pulled around the corner out of sight of the last car that had to be the coach's.

We waited for hours for the coach to come out and claim the car we had been watching. The sun had already gone down below the horizon and it was beginning to get dark. Suddenly the streetlights switched on. I could still feel the strange feeling in my chest and knew the coach was still in the building. I sent Dakota a quick message knowing that he was rising for the night. I thought to myself how great it would be for him to be with us during the day. A short time later I heard the sound of a motorcycle screaming down the highway. I watched Dakota pull up behind us in the rearview mirror.

"What's up? Dakota said as I rolled down my window.

"We are waiting on the coach to leave the school. We are going to follow him and see if we can catch him doing anything weird," I explained.

"That's his car?" Dakota asked.

"We're pretty sure. It's the only one left and he hasn't come out yet," I replied.

"Hang on a second," Dakota said as he pulled something out of his pocket.

He showed us the little square object in his hand. It looked like some kind of computer chip.

"Never leave home without 'em," Dakota said smiling just before taking off at vampire speed.

In the blink of an eye Dakota was crouched down behind the coach's car. We continued to watch as he reached under the back of it. When he was done with what he was doing he was instantly back at my window still smiling.

"What was that?" Ava asked.

I was going to ask the same thing, only Ava got to it before I could.

"It's a tracking chip Dante gave me a while back. Didn't you guys get some?" Dakota asked showing the flashing red dot on the screen of his cell phone.

"No we didn't!" Matt exclaimed from the back seat. "But that is so cool!"

"Pull it up on your computer, Luke," Dakota said.

He reached through the window to the screen in the dash and punched a few buttons. Suddenly the same flashing red dot showed up like the one

"There he is!" Ava exclaimed.

"Let's go!" I said turning to look out at Dakota. But, he was no longer there.

I heard the bike crank behind us and knew he was ready. We watched as the coach got into his car and pulled out of the parking lot. Luckily he headed in the opposite direction from where we were sitting.

I let the dot get a few blocks ahead of us before I pulled out and started following. I didn't want to risk getting spotted by the coach. I waited until the strange feeling started to fade before we started moving. We followed for several miles to an area on the outskirts of town. I had never been to this area. There were very few houses that I spotted as I continued to follow. Once we made it completely out of town I increased the distance between us and the coach and just followed the tracking system. I switched off my headlights and a few seconds later I noticed Dakota turned his off as well. Ava was the only one that seemed nervous about driving in the pitch dark. The rest of the people in the vehicle, I knew, could see perfectly well. Ava reached over and squeezed my hand.

I watched on the screen as the car slowed down and made a turn. I slowed down myself before reaching the road and pulled over onto the shoulder. The turn the car had made was a driveway. We watched for a couple minutes as the car pulled down slowly and stopped about three hundred yards from where we were now parked. The strange feeling remained strong in my chest.

"We need to get closer," I said as I quickly climbed out of the car.

I went to the trunk and pulled out my sword. I put it in place on my back and was instantly transformed to my white uniform. Once everyone joined me we watched as Matt and Jenna both shifted into their wolf forms. Matt took off ahead of us into the woods. After a few minutes Jenna shifted back to her normal self.

"Matt sees the house. He watched the coach go in. Follow me," Jenna said as she quickly shifted back to wolf and headed into the woods after Matt. I knew she could smell him as we followed her. It wasn't long before we came to Matt. He had shifted and was squatting down in the wood line looking at a small run down shack.

"I know they have to be paying the coach more than that!" Matt said motioning toward the nearly inhabitable little house.

"His car looks like is cost more than that house," said Dakota.

"We can't see what's going on in there. What was the point in even coming out here?" asked Ava.

I knew she was right so I did the only thing that came to my mind. I turned and started walking straight for the house. The strange feeling remained strong in my chest. It even got stronger the closer I got to the house. I walked in the shadows to make sure I wouldn't be spotted out one of the windows. My plan was to go over and pull a peeking tom to see what was happening in the house.

There was only one window with a very dim light coming from it. Once I made it close enough I saw the coach standing in what appeared to be the living room. There was no furniture, only a few lit candles sitting on the floor around the room. The coach raised his hands above his head and in a flash he disappeared right before my eyes. He wasn't the only thing that disappeared. The strange feeling I had felt for the past few hours was completely gone too.

I threw my hands in the air in defeat and quickly turned to find the rest of the group standing right behind me.

"He disappeared!" I exclaimed.

"Well, I guess it's safe to say he isn't human," Matt said casually.

"What do we do now?" asked Jenna.

"Not much we can do right?" asked Dakota.

"You must not know me very well," said Ava as she pulled out one of her yellow transport spells we had used to follow the troll not long ago.

"Looks like we follow him," said Jenna as she turned and made her way to the front door.

We all followed Jenna to the front door as she took the lead. She pushed the door open slowly and stepped inside. She slowly made her way inside once she was sure the coast was clear. All of a sudden Jordan appeared out of thin air. We all gasped from her sudden presence.

"What are you doing here?" I whispered as if we were hiding from somebody.

"We got tired of waiting for you guys to get home so I decided to come look for you. And why are you whispering?" Jordan asked.

"We are following the coach," said Ava.

"Why are you following a coach?" asked Jordan with a puzzled look on her face.

"We don't have time for this," said Jenna.

"She's right. The portal he used can only be accessed for a short time," said Ava.

"You guys are on a mission and didn't even call us," said Jordan. I could tell she was a little hurt by not being included.

"It was a last minute decision. There wasn't time to call anybody. And, there still isn't," I told her.

We needed to get going before we missed our chance. We all circled around where the coach had been standing moments ago. We watched patiently as Ava brought her hand holding the spell into the air. She quickly threw the spell at the floor smashing it open. Suddenly everything went black.

"Is everybody here?" I asked.

It was so dark I could barely see myself, even with my extremely heightened senses. I looked around slowly trying to figure out where we were. Just about the time I realized we were in some kind of large dome shaped room my blood chilled sending a shiver down my spine. The strange feeling was nearly clawing its way out of my chest. The feeling had never been this strong before.

Suddenly dozens of sets of blue eyes began to light up like large blue stars in the night sky.

"Ava," can you please get us out of here," I whispered as quietly as I could.

"Yes please, like NOW!" I heard Jenna exclaim as she raised her hands into the air.

"Jenna, DON"T!" I yelled, just as her hands began to glow nearly the same blue as the eyes staring back at us.

As the light radiated up onto the ceiling we were finally able to really see what was surrounding us. The most hideous looking creatures held the glowing blue eyes completely filling up the ceiling like a jigsaw puzzle. It was hard to tell where one creature ended and the other began.

In a matter of seconds after Ava threw the spell we were again standing in the same spot back at the coach's house. We all jumped as five large thumps hit the roof right above our heads.

"What the…?" said Matt.

"I agree, what was that?" asked Jenna.

"Oh, no!" Ava exclaimed.

"What exactly do you mean when by oh, no?" asked Dakota.

"I think we might have brought a few of those things back with us," said Ava.

Suddenly the most awful noise I had ever heard in my life erupted from outside on the roof. It was as if the creatures were screaming in agony. Luckily it stopped just as quickly as it started. But, what replaced it was even worse. Suddenly the house started to shake violently as if there was an earthquake.

"We need to get out of here," I said over the sound of the wood protesting against the sudden movement.

"But those things are out there," said Ava.

"I know, but they are going to bring down this old place on top of us," I told her.

"Jordan, can you jump us outside?" I asked.

"I think so," Jordan said. I could hear her voice trembling a little and knew she was scared.

Something suddenly crashed through the roof and landed a short distance from us. The creature jumped quickly to its four claw-like feet. It turned around and began snarling at us as it crouched for an attack. I drew my sword as I moved to stand between the creature and my team. The creature suddenly pounced like a cat and sliced one of its razor sharp claws at me. It barely cut through my jacket sleeve, as I brought my sword down to slice off its whole leg. I watched in horror as the cat like creature stumbled back a few steps and screamed out in pain.

Just as the creature regained its balance, to my utmost shock, the whole arm I had just cut off had magically grown back good as new. I was at a loss for words as pain began shooting through the scratch the creature caused on my arm.

"What are you waiting for?" I heard Jenna scream.

A few seconds later we were standing outside the house close to the wood line where we were before.

"What are we going to do?" asked Dakota.

I could tell he had become worried after seeing the sudden regeneration of the creature's limb. Honestly, I couldn't think of a single thing to do. I knew, however, that we couldn't let these things escape into the city.

"I have an idea," said Matt.

We all turned quickly to look at him. We eagerly waited for him to tell us what he was thinking. We watched as he quickly backed away from us a short distance and then instantly shifted into the huge dragon we had become familiar with. With a few beats of his enormous wings he was high in the air above us. Our eyes were glued to him as he positioned himself over the little shack and let out a huge jet of fire straight toward the horrifying black creatures. To our amazement the creatures had a weakness and we had finally learned what it was.

The pain in my arm was growing stronger with every beat of my heart. Another surge of pain shot through my entire body bringing me to my knees.

"Luke what's wrong?" Matt said as he ran to my side. "I watched you go down from the air."

Everyone was focused on the flames shooting out of the shacks old worn out roof and didn't notice that I had went down.

"Luke!" shouted Ava as she too ran to my side.

Just then there was a loud crash from the direction of the shack. Everyone turned quickly to see what it was making all the noise. Unfortunately, nobody liked what they saw. A set of blue eyes glowed back at us from the hideous black creature that had escaped through the window of the house. It screamed its deafening cry as it crashed its way out of the house and landed between us and the house.

"I've got this!" Ava proclaimed as she stood to her feet.

We all were trembling as the creature started galloping toward us. I watched in amazement as Ava lifted her hands toward the creature that was quickly closing the distance toward attacking us. Suddenly, as the creature leapt into the air to pounce on us, three balls of fire shot from Ava's raised hands. The fare balls connected with the creature in mid air. One last scream from the creature ended in a ball of black dust that rained to the ground like snow.

I was proud that Ava and Matt had single handedly taken down four of these mysterious creatures. Creatures that seemed to be the only ones capable of causing me pain. I blacked out before I was able to thank Ava and Matt for protecting the soldiers. One little scratch and I was surprisingly down and out. I didn't think I even had any weaknesses, but unfortunately that wasn't true. In less than a month I had been taken down twice by two different creatures.

16

I only remember waking up one time. I woke up to terrible pain and something being poured down my throat before I passed out again. The second time I woke up the pain was surprisingly gone, and Ava sat on my bed beside me smiling back at me.

"How long was I out?" I asked.

"Only a couple hours," she replied.

Wow! I thought to myself. I felt like I had been asleep for days I was so lightheaded. I didn't know what a hangover felt like but I would have to say that's the only thing that could compare to how I felt.

"Dr. Blevins tested the venom in your wound," Ava said as I looked down to see my arm was completely healed. "It was the same as the last time you were injured. I remembered what you told me healed you," she said motioning toward the counter of the bar.

I looked over and instantly spotted the bottle of blood. I closed my eyes as everything she had said sank in. I couldn't quite seem to put all the pieces together. What did the elf and the horrific creatures we battled have in common? And, how was the new coach involved in all of this? These were the questions I kept asking myself.

"You should get some rest, Luke. I have school in the morning so I need to go to bed myself," Ava said snapping me back to reality.

"I'm sorry, Ava. I am just so sleepy I guess I can't even hold my eyes open," I said.

"Good night, Luke. I'll see you first thing in the morning," Ava said just before she leaned over and kissed me.

"I love you," I said.

"I love you too," said Ava as she stood and walked out of the room.

I fell back on my pillow hard and let out a long sigh. I threw the covers back and immediately realized I was naked again. My face blushed red as I wondered why they saw it necessary to strip me when all of my wounds had been above the waist. I found it quite disturbing actually.

When I stood up, I spotted the bottle sitting on the counter. I walked over and poured myself a glass. I used the same one Ava had used earlier to pour some into my mouth to heal me. I quickly downed the entire glass before putting everything away. I went to the bathroom and took a quick shower before crawling back into my warm bed. In no time at all I was sound asleep.

When I woke up the next morning I felt completely rested. Something that had nothing to do with the recent events popped into my head as soon as I was awake. Jonathan had asked me to talk Mike into leading the Little Rock coven of vampires. It was his one condition in the decision to take my place as leader of the England coven. I looked at my clock and realized it was nearly noon. I was glad I had gotten to sleep in and not have to get up and go to school. I showered and threw on some clothes before heading downstairs to see what was going on in regards to the search for my parents.

When I reached the bottom of the stairs there was a sudden surge of the now familiar feeling in the center of my chest. I didn't quite know what was causing it, but I had learned to associate it with bad. Every time I felt it, I encountered someone or something evil. I couldn't understand why there would be something evil invading the mansion. The feeling led me to the Great Room as I quickly opened the door to see what was causing it.

"Good morning, Luke!" exclaimed Grandpa as he walked over to meet me. He pulled me into a big bear hug.

I hugged Grandpa back but I didn't take my eyes off of his guest that was sitting at the conference table. The man smiled back at me as though he knew me.

"Who is that?" I asked.

"Luke, this is Mr. Bryce. He is one of the council's detectives. He will be handling the investigation into your mother's kidnapping," explained Grandpa.

The man continued to smile as he extended his hand inviting me to shake it. I didn't want to be rude to Grandpa's guest, but I almost didn't even want to touch the man. The strange feeling continued to pulse through my chest.

I reluctantly shook his hand, but I never broke eye contact through the entire meeting. We all sat down at the table as the man began explaining that he had experience dealing with the dark one in the past. He told us how he chased the dark elf all over the world that through several different dimensions. He said he even caught the elf several times, but somehow he always seemed to escape.

"He want escape this time," I told the man confidently.

The man looked at me puzzled by my sudden interruption in his story.

"What do you mean?" asked Mr. Bryce.

"I want allow him to escape this time. He will not get out alive," I explained.

I noticed the man's expression changed suddenly from his puzzled look to a look of surprise at what I was saying.

"I hope you are right, Luke," said Mr. Bryce.

I was trying my best not to be rude, but I couldn't shake the feeling I had in my chest. Nothing good had come from this feeling, and I didn't think it was going to change with Mr. Bryce. I also knew we needed as much help as we could get finding my mother whether the man was evil or not.

The man continued to talk about the dark elf. He used lots of big words about profiling and such. I had no idea what he was talking about most of the time. Grandpa shook his head as though he accepted everything Mr. Bryce was telling us. Once he was done talking, he dismissed himself to "get to work" finding my kidnapped parents.

"Luke, I really don't appreciate you being rude to our guests. Especially not ones that come from the council. What has gotten in to you?" Grandpa asked.

I started telling Grandpa about the strange feelings I had been having. The soldiers were the only other ones that I had told about it. I knew Grandpa was disappointed I had been hiding things from him by the expression on his face. But, once I told him about having the same feeling with Mr. Bryce his expression was more on the side of anger.

"Luke, why are you hiding things from me now?" asked Grandpa.

"I'm sorry Grandpa. I don't mean to hide things. Its just that I am always so busy dealing with all the stuff that keeps happening that I can't really remember who I tell what," I lied.

There probably were things that I forgot to tell him, but some things I felt I just needed to keep to myself for some reason.

"You know you can tell me anything, right?" asked Grandpa.

"Of course I do, Grandpa," I said smiling at him.

Grandpa smiled back and reached over to squeeze my shoulder.

"You are turning into a fine young man, Luke," he said.

"Thanks, Grandpa. There is something else I actually came down to talk to you about," I said.

"Ok, Luke. What's up?" Grandpa asked.

"Well, you remember one of Jonathan's conditions for taking the position in England was to talk Professor Vance into leading the Little Rock coven. I need you to help me talk to him," I explained.

"It's already taken care of. I talked to Mr. Vance as soon as we got back from England," Grandpa said.

"Really? That's great!" I exclaimed.

I was glad that the issue had already been handled. I wondered if Mike actually wanted the position, or if Grandpa asked him to fill it.

"I have some business I need to see about, Luke," Grandpa said.

"Ok. I'll see you later, Grandpa," I said.

As we were leaving the room back into the lobby my phone sounded. It was a message from Walter Johnson. Walter was a scientist that worked in my building back in England. I quickly opened the message and read.

"I did it! I finally finished the serum. I'm on my way to your house. I will be there in half an hour," the message said.

"Ok, see you then," I replied.

I went to the kitchen to grab a bite to eat while I waited for Walter to arrive. I wondered what was so important that Walter felt the need to rush half way across the world. When I finished eating I headed back out into the lobby where Walter was just arriving at the mansion.

"Hey Walter, what's up? I asked.

"Can we go somewhere more private?" he asked.

"Sure," I said as I led him toward headquarters.

I watched as Walter nervously hugged a briefcase to his chest as if he was protecting it with his life. He followed me downstairs and into the small conference room.

"What's wrong Walter? You traveled half way around the world for this. You are kind of worrying me a little bit," I said.

Walter walked over to the table and sat the briefcase down. He entered the combination and opened the case quickly.

"I did it!" he exclaimed.

"Did what?" I asked not really know what I was looking at.

The case was filled with probably two dozen small vials, each filled with a clear liquid. I watched as Walter pulled one of the vials out and showed it to me as though it would make me know what it was.

"It's the serum! This will make any vampire be able to go out in daylight. Do you know what this means?" Walter asked.

I still wasn't catching on to what he was so nervous about.

"I don't guess I do, Walter," I said.

"Luke, if anybody finds out this serum even exists, every vampire on the planet will do anything necessary to get it," Walter explained.

"That could definitely be a problem," I said suddenly understand the importance of what Walter had brought to the mansion.

I immediately send Grandpa a message and in a few minutes he was hustling into the room.

"What's wrong, Luke?" Grandpa asked in his most worried tone.

I listened as Walter explained everything about the serum. He told us that this was the only batch that had been created so far. He also said the only copy of the formula was saved on the hard drive he showed us was also in the case.

"Who else knows about this?" Grandpa asked.

"Only the three of us," Walter replied.

"We need to keep it that way until we figure out what to do with it," said Grandpa.

"I agree. We don't want to have all of the vampires out scouring the country for this," I said.

"Why don't we put this in the vault, Luke? It should be safe there for the time being," said Grandpa.

"That sounds like a good idea," I said suddenly getting nervous about even having it at the mansion.

"I have something else to show you, Luke," said Walter as he closed up the case and handed it to Grandpa.

"Ok. Let's see it," I said.

"We have to go outside first," Walter said smiling.

Grandpa headed to the vault with the serum while Walter and I headed for the elevator. We walked through the lobby and out the front door and I immediately found out what it was Walter wanted to show me.

The machine sitting in the driveway definitely was not a car. It was about the size of a car but looked more like some type of rocket. It sat on three small wheels and had small wings like a plane. It was solid black with a dome shaped glass window covering the top of it and tinted so dark you couldn't see inside. It was like something you see in a science fiction movie flying through space.

"What is it? I asked as I walked around the machine looking at it from all angles. It was one of the coolest things I had ever seen.

"I call it a Travelport!" Walter said excitedly. "It's just like teleporting, only not quite as fast. Want to take it for a spin?"

"Sure, but I don't know how to drive it," I said excitedly.

Walter walked over to the side of the machine and pushed a small button. The window raised up a few inches and slid toward the back of the Travelport revealing two seats, one behind the other.

"You don't drive it. All you have to do is tell it where to go," Walter said.

I quickly climbed in and looked at the single computer like screen sitting in front of me. Walter climbed in the seat behind me.

"Just touch the screen, Luke," Walter said.

I touched the screen and it lit up. I heard a voice ask "What is your destination?"

"Take us to Stallings Incorporated," I heard Walter say from the back seat.

"Wait, I don't have time to fly to England!" I said as the window slid shut. The machine began to vibrate softly and raised up off the ground several feet.

"Just wait, we will be back before you know it," Walter said as the machine continued to rise up higher into the sky and rotate around slowly.

The Travelport suddenly shot forward. It took off so fast my head was slammed back against the leather headrest. In a fraction of a second we were streaking through the air so fast the world around us was only a blur. In a matter of minutes the Travelport started to slow down. I also noticed the machine was going down lower toward the ground. When we cleared the clouds I could see that we were heading down toward the roof of my building in England. We touched down and the window opened for us to get out.

"That was awesome!" I exclaimed as I jumped out of the Travelport onto the roof.

"I knew you would like it," Walter said proudly.

"When can I get one?" I asked.

I wanted one of these for myself no matter how much it cost. I watched Walter as he reached to his wrist and unfastened his watch. He threw it to me and I caught it in mid air.

"It's all yours, Luke. I work for you, buddy, remember?" Walter asked.

"Dude, that's great! Is it really mine?" I asked excitedly.

"Of course, Luke," said Walter.

"You could make billions selling these things, Walter!"

"Yes we can!" Walter said smiling.

I suddenly realized that, since Walter worked for me, I was more or less in control of his inventions. The possibilities seemed to be endless with two of the most amazing inventions of all time. What would Walter come up with next? I couldn't wait to find out.

Walter showed me how to manually drive the Travelport once it was on the ground. It would allow me to park it inside headquarters back at the mansion. He even showed me that I could call the Travelport to wherever I was using the watch he gave me. I hadn't planned to go to England that day, but since I was there I decided to go down and check on Jonathan and my business. Walter rode down the elevator with me. I got off on the floor where my office was located. Walter said goodbye and headed back down to his lab in the basement.

Jonathan of course was down for the day. He wouldn't rise until dark. I don't know why that hadn't occurred to me sooner. It really was annoying having to wait until dark for my vampire friends to rise before I could talk to them. I decided I wasn't going to wait around and headed back to the roof to go back home.

When I got back to the mansion and drove the Travelport into headquarters I noticed Matt, Jenna, and Ava getting out of Matt's truck. I realized they had just made it home from school. Their mouths all hung open in amazement as they watched me pull into a parking spot next to them.

"Luke! What is that? Can I drive it? That is so cool!" Matt exclaimed as the window slid open revealing me as the driver.

"I'll take you for a ride later, Matt. I want to hear about what happened with the coach," I told him.

Ava walked over me and kissed me for several seconds before she would let me go. She grinned from ear to ear up at me.

"Wow!" was all I could say.

"Let's go upstairs and we can tell you everything!" Ava said.

I couldn't imagine what had Ava in such a good mood.

That is the first time I have seen you smile in weeks!" she said as she took my hand and led me toward the elevator.

When we made it to my room upstairs everybody took their normal spots around the fireplace. I started by explaining the events of my day. From the weird detective from the council all the way through the amazing experience I had going to England and back in about a half hour.

"That is so awesome!" Matt said. I knew he was more than a little excited about getting to ride in the Travelport.

"So, tell me what I missed at school," I said.

"Well, the weirdest thing ever happened today," started Ava.

"Yeah, the coach didn't even show up. He just left us these notes in our lockers. There was one in yours too," Matt said handing me an envelope.

I looked at the writing on the front. It had my name written in a beautiful cursive script. I opened it to see what the coach had written.

"You see what happens when you go following people? If you are reading this my plans for your immediate destruction failed miserably. How did you like my babies? Are they not the most fun you ever had? I advise you to STOP FOLLOWING ME, if you know what is good for you. Next time there is no telling what you will jump yourself into!" said the letter.

I looked up questioningly at the rest of my friends. I waited for somebody to explain.

"Those were in all of our lockers. But, the weird part was the coach wasn't at school today," said Ava.

"You will never guess who showed up instead!" exclaimed Jenna.

"Who?" I asked.

"The old coach!" exclaimed Matt.

"He just showed up like nothing ever happened. No explanation about where he had been, or who the other coach was. I think it is safe to say that James Doyle is gone for good," said Ava.

"I can't believe nobody even notices that we had a different coach for several weeks," I said.

"The only thing we can figure is that he used some sort of spell on the minds of the humans," said Ava.

"It is amazing how easily a human's mind can be manipulated," said Jenna.

"Hey! I'm one of those humans!" Ava exclaimed.

"I didn't mean you, Ava. You are an exception to the rule of course," said Jenna.

"There has to be something we can do. Are we supposed to just forget that he tried to kill us?" I asked.

"I think him leading us to that cave full of monsters was just part of his plan," said Ava.

"What do you mean? I asked.

"Well, look at what we know so far. You get shot by the dark elf and nearly die from the strange venom on the arrow he used. Then the coach leads us into a cave full of the monsters where that venom comes from. Don't you think there has to be something linking the two together somehow?" asked Ava.

I don't know why I hadn't realized it sooner. I guessed with everything else going on I hadn't really put the pieces together. Somehow the dark elf and the coach were connected.

"So the coach and the elf are connected somehow?" asked Jenna.

"I believe so. I don't think its a coincidence that we encountered the same poison with both of them. And that it just happens to be a poison that can hurt Luke," said Ava.

"I think Ava may be on to something," I said.

"But what can we do about it?" asked Matt.

"Nothing," I said quietly.

I knew there was nothing we could do. My parents had been missing for days and there seemed to be nothing anybody could do to find them. Not even the council itself was able to locate the dark one. A single tear escaped my eye as I attempted to hold myself together. I could have burst into tears as I thought about my mother. Would I ever see her again?

17

My mind was racing as I though about everything that was currently happening in my life. I tried to shake the feeling of helplessness but it seemed to be no use. I stood up and walked over to the refrigerator to pour myself a glass of blood. I took a sip before turning back toward my friends. They all stared back at me with disgusted looks plastered on their faces.

"What?" I asked. "Why are you staring at me like I've got two heads or something?"

"That's seriously gross, man!" Matt exclaimed.

"But it's not gross to chomp down on a live animal?" I asked him.

We usually always hunted while we were running in wolf form. I didn't see how drinking blood was any worse than raw meat and hair.

"I guess you got me with that one," Matt said.

Just as I was about to walk back to my seat my vision went black and I crashed to the floor spilling the glass of blood in the process. The vision was the same as before. Nhados stands there smiling holding a newborn baby. The scene flashes and Nhados is still standing there only this time he doesn't have a baby. Standing next to him is a young boy probably three years old give or take.

I woke up soaked in the blood I was carrying. It looked as though I had been attacked. My friends were crouched around me knowing exactly what had just happened.

"What did you see, Luke?" asked Matt.

I explained the vision was the same as before. About the baby and the boy with Nhados. Nobody seemed to have any kind of explanation about the vision. I wondered who's child Nhados could be holding.

After my friends helped me get the blood all cleaned up, Matt was anxious to go back down and ride in the Travelport. I wanted to get my mind off of things so I agreed.

"Where do you want to go?" I asked Matt as we watched the window close and lock in place around us.

I drove the Travelport out of headquarters and into the warm evening sunshine.

"What is your destination?" said the computer voice.

"Take us to my dad," said Matt.

I think he was more talking to me instead of the computer. The Travelport immediately started vibrating and rising to the air like it had before. Once we were high enough we shout forward like a bullet from a gun. In a matter of seconds we were slowing back down and descending into the familiar neighborhood where Matt and I grew up. We slowly went down and landed right in our old driveway right behind Uncle Charles's truck.

"Why is your dad in Dallas?" I asked.

"He came here on business. He must be staying at the house while he works here," said Matt.

The window slid open and we both jumped out. I was kind of excited getting to see our old house once again. The front door was unlocked, so we let ourselves in. we both stopped dead in our tracks as soon as we made it in the living room. Matt's dad was sitting on the couch making out with a woman we had never seen before. The two jumped apart as if they were kids being caught by their parents.

"Alright Dad!" Matt exclaimed. "I wondered if you were ever going to get a girlfriend. You didn't have to hide out in Dallas to do it though."

"Matt what are you doing here?" asked Uncle Charles.

"Well we were trying out Luke's new flying machine and decided to come see you," said Matt excitedly.

"Ha ha ha," Uncle Charles laughed as he jumped up off of the couch. "Kids and their overactive imagination," he added smiling at the woman on the couch.

He quickly proceeded to push us back out the front door.

"You can't talk like that in front of her guys," Uncle Charles whispered where only we could hear him. "Oh my gosh you have got to get that thing out of here. She might see it," he said once the door was securely closed behind us.

"What's the big deal? It's not like she's human or something," said Matt.

Uncle Charles only stared at Matt. We waited for him to say something but after several seconds Matt's eyes began to get big.

"You're dating a human?" Matt asked a little louder than necessary. "All the hot single moms that are in and out of the mansion and you pick a human? I see why you decided to keep her a big secret now."

"Matt you don't understand. It's not like that. Please give me a chance to explain. I will be home tomorrow. Let's make time to talk about this. I'll explain everything. But, right now I really need you to get this thing out of the driveway," Uncle Charles pleaded.

"I love you son," Uncle Charles called out to Matt. Matt had turned around and headed toward the Travelport without another word to his father. "Please don't be upset. I promise I can explain."

I didn't think it was a big deal that he was dating a human. I wondered why Matt was so upset by it. I shrugged my shoulders at Uncle Charles letting him know I had no idea why Matt was acting the way he was. I followed Matt and climbed in the front seat. I waved at Uncle Charles as the window closed around us.

"Take us home!" Matt said before the computer voice could even ask.

"Matt, what got into you? Why were you so mean to your dad?" I asked as the vehicle began to vibrate.

"How could he date a human? Why would he even want to? And on top of everything else, she doesn't even know about us!" shouted Matt from the back seat.

"Matt, please calm down. There must be a logical explanation as to the reasons around the relationship. I agree he probably should have told her about the supernatural world by now, but I bet he will be able to explain everything tomorrow. If he is traveling all the way to Dallas to see her, he must really love her. At least give him the chance to tell you about her before you pass judgment," I said.

Matt remained silent behind me as the Travelport suddenly rocketed back toward the mansion. I knew he was thinking about what I said. When the window opened to let us out Matt jumped out and headed toward the elevator. When he was nearly there I used my speed to block his path.

"Get out of the way!" Matt ordered.

I really did not like the way he was talking to me much at all.

"Matt, why are you acting like this?" I asked.

"Why are you taking his side? I thought you were my best friend," Matt said.

"I'm not taking anybody's side, Matt. I just want you to find out the whole story before you make a decision about it," I said.

"Just move out of the way," said Matt as he attempted to push me out of his way. I gently pushed him off of me causing him to take several steps backward.

Really? You think you can just push me around?" I asked. "You know you don't stand a chance against me, Matt."

"That's what you think!" Matt yelled as he used his speed and strength to close the distance between us and shove me into the elevator behind us.

"Are you really going to do this?" I asked.

Matt actually had the courage to growl at me as he continued to pin me against the now dented elevator doors. But, before he had time to react I reached up and grabbed the front of his shirt and threw him through the air causing him to crash into the concrete wall on the other side of the room. Small bits of debris flew off the wall and landed on the floor along with Matt.

"You're gonna pay for that, Luke," said Matt as he began to transform into the familiar black wolf.

"Matt, please don't do this," I tried to plead with him.

I knew there was no way he could take me. But, I didn't want to end up hurting him in the process of proving it. I watched as Matt suddenly started sprinting toward me. I waited until he made it to about the middle of the room before I jumped into action. I ran toward Matt at top speed grabbing him by the throat with one hand. In one swift movement I slammed him down to the floor. I heard him whine as his body made contact with the floor.

The more he struggled to get away, the harder I squeezed the death grip I had on his neck. I held him there pinned to the floor with nearly no effort on my part. I could have just as easily been holding down a small puppy. He started whining again before he finally stopped struggling all together.

I heard the elevator doors open and quickly turned to see who it was. I guessed the guy taking Dante's place in the security booth had told Grandpa what was happening because he stormed off the elevator toward us.

"Luke! Matt! What do you think you are doing?" Grandpa shouted at us as he continued to stomp toward us. Each time one of his expensive shoes hit the floor it echoed throughout the entire large room.

I looked down and realized Matt had shifted back to his human self and was now glaring up at me as I continued to pin him to the floor.

"Get up! Both of you!" Grandpa continued to shout at us. "I thought you boys were more mature than this."

I could hear the disappointment in his voice. I never wanted any altercation with Matt. This was all his fault. I probably could have handled it a little different, but Matt started it. I slowly released my grip on his neck and say the makings of bruises in the shape of my handprints. I immediately was sorry I had hurt him. But, he needed to be put in his place.

"All you had to do was get out of my way!" Matt said as he picked himself up off the floor.

"You shouldn't treat your friends like that, Matt. And you certainly don't disrespect your family by attacking them," I told him.

I didn't have anything else to say as I turned and walked toward the elevator. I left Grandpa to deal with Matt and his little temper tantrum. I went straight to my room texting Ava on the way to tell her good night. I wasn't in the mood to talk to anybody tonight.

I fell asleep fairly quickly. The same dream of Nhados and the baby started along with the young boy. I wondered if the baby and the boy might be the same person. The dream made no sense to me.

The next morning I was woke up by the strange feeling in my chest. I got up and jumped in the shower. I had a good idea about who was causing the feeling this early in the morning. I got dressed and headed downstairs to meet the man from the council. I hoped he had news about the search for my parents. Before I made it to the bottom of the stairs the feeling started to fade and I knew he was leaving the mansion. When I made it into the lobby Grandpa was coming in the front door.

"Good morning, Grandpa. I'm really sorry about last night," I told him.

"You boys need to work out whatever differences you are having," Grandpa said. I didn't want to talk about the issues Matt was having so I changed the subject.

"Was that the man from the council?" I asked.

"It was, actually, but how did you know?" Grandpa asked.

"I heard his voice," I lied. I don't know why, but I chose not to tell anybody about the strange feeling I was having about the man. "Any news about Mom?" I asked hopefully.

"He came to let me know that the dark one had been spotted several times. They can't pinpoint his location because sightings are coming up on different continents around the world. He is never seen in one place more than once," said Grandpa.

"Oh," I said sadly.

"You would think with all the resources the council has in their power that they would be able to do more to find him," said Grandpa. "I have always thought the council was useless."

I never knew Grandpa felt so strongly against the council. I always thought he was with them as he explained different rules to me over the years. After all, the soldiers enforced many of the laws that he explained to us. But, I agreed that the council should have been able to find them by now.

Grandpa left me alone in the lobby to work in his office so I decided to go to the dining hall and eat before everybody else got up. We had the day off from school for parent teacher conferences, and I couldn't wait for Uncle Charles to come and tell us about his new girlfriend. I hoped Matt had calmed himself down some by now.

As I was finishing breakfast the rest of the group came in. Ava, Jenna, and Matt took their normal places around me. I noticed Matt wouldn't even look at me.

"Good morning," I said as they sat down.

"Good morning, Luke," Ava said as she leaned over and kissed me.

"Good morning," said Jenna.

Matt remained silent. I couldn't believe he wasn't even going to tell me good morning. My anger at his foolishness started to build again.

"Tell him!" Jenna exclaimed as she elbowed Matt right in his stomach.

"I'm sorry," Matt said so quietly we barely heard what he said.

"Louder!" Jenna said again driving her elbow into the same spot causing him to exhale suddenly.

"Ok! Ok! I'm sorry, Luke. I shouldn't have attacked you last night. It won't happen again," Matt said.

I was thankful Matt had apologized, but the tone he used said he didn't really mean it. I guessed Jenna wore the pants in that relationship though. I figured she was forcing him to say he was sorry. I accepted his apology even though I could tell it was a fake. I could only hope that he would come around and get over whatever issues he was having.

"What do you guys have planned for today?" I asked.

Nobody said anything as they shook their heads unable to think of any plans.

"Nothing really," said Jenna.

"No, not really, I can't think of anything," said Matt.

"What about you?" Ava asked.

"I haven't heard from Eric and his crew lately. I thought about checking on them today," I said.

"I talked to Katie yesterday. She said they have been training day and night since they got here. When they are not training they are sleeping," Jenna said.

"Eric said they hope to get their training finished so they can go home. He said him and Katie need to get back to school," Matt said.

"Why don't we go down and see what they are up to?" I asked.

"I have some things I need to take care of first. I'll meet you down there later," said Ava.

We parted ways with Ava and made our way down to headquarters. We passed the security desk and the little man working it seemed to get nervous when he saw Matt and I together again. I guessed he hadn't forgotten about last night either. When we made it down toward the end of the room we could hear something going on in the training room. Loud thuds and grunts echoed through the large room. We walked through the door just as Jordan swung Patrick through the air and pinned him to the mat.

"I give up!" pleaded Patrick as he lay on his back on the floor. His sister, Jordan, held him there effortlessly.

"Hey, Luke, what do you say about giving me a little competition?" asked Jordan.

"Yeah, and give me a break," said Patrick still pinned to the mat.

Jordan stood up pulling Patrick up off his feet with ease. He walked away from her quickly before she could get her hands on him again.

"Don't be scared. I will go easy on you," Jordan said teasing me out onto the wrestling mat.

"I will probably be the one that has to go easy," I said giggling at her.

"We'll just have to see about that," Jordan said as she made the first move.

Jordan sprinted across the mat at vampire speed. I easily stepped out of the way long before she made contact.

"You're pretty fast, Luke. But, can you do this?" Jordan said as she suddenly disappeared.

In the blink of an eye I felt arms wrap around me from behind. I was flipped through the air and slammed to the mat. Jordan had me pinned.

"Aw you sneaky devil!" I said as I smiled up at her.

I quickly swung my legs around pulling my top half out of her grip pushing her face down into the mat. I pulled her arms around behind her back as if I was a cop and she was under arrest. The only thing missing was the handcuffs. Jordan again disappeared. She was instantly standing on the other side of the mat from me.

"You give up?" I asked her as I continued to give her my evilest of grins.

"Not on your life!" she said excitedly.

She blinked again and was standing right in front of me. She reached out to grab me and I easily blocked her arm. She tried again and again with no luck. I blocked her movement every time. I even showed off a bit and only used one hand to block her attacks. I used the other hand to pat my mouth as I let out a fake yawn taunting her. Our arms and legs moved so fast that I doubted anyone else in the room could even see as she continued to throw attacks and I continued to block them.

Finally she gave up and took a few steps backward crossing her arms over her chest as though she was going to pout about losing.

"You are really good, Luke," said Jordan. "I think I finally met my match."

I just laughed. She knew as well as I did that she was no match for my speed and strength. Even with her ability to disappear I doubted she would be able to take me.

"How is the training coming? I asked the group.

"Well, we finished our supernatural studies pretty quick. We had learned most of it already so it was easy to progress pretty fast. A couple more nights with Professor Vance and I believe we will be ready. He only has a few more techniques he wants us to go over," explained Eric.

"That's great! You guys will be up and running before you know it." I said.

I was excited to learn that the England unit of the Silent Soldiers was nearing its completion. I thought to myself it was one of many Silent Soldiers teams I had plans to create. With the new Travelport machine making it easy for intercontinental travel, and teams strategically placed all over the world, we would easily be able to ward off bad guys and uphold the laws of the council.

Matt and Jenna decided to hand out with the new soldiers for a while. I had a few things I needed to see about myself. As I headed up onto the elevator the strange feeling returned in my chest. As I came off the elevator the feeling went away just as quickly as it appeared. I thought to myself how strange it was. I blew it off not really knowing what to think about it.

As I walked through the lobby Uncle Charles came in the front door.

"Hey Uncle Charles," I said.

"Hey. Do you know where Matt is? I really need to talk to you boys," he said. I could tell he was nervous from the events about talking to us after the way Matt acted the evening before.

"He is downstairs. I'll let him know you are here," I said pulling my phone out. I sent him a message to come up as Uncle Charles and I headed for the great room so he could talk to us. A few minutes later Matt came in.

"Dad, I am very sorry about how I acted yesterday," Matt said as he walked up to his dad and hugged him.

What was up with him? Yesterday when I tried to talk to him he attacked me. And today he is apologizing? I could tell the apology to his dad was more sincere than the one he gave me at breakfast.

"No, Matt, Luke, I am the one that should be sorry. I should have told you about me and Susan years ago," said Uncle Charles. "Sit down and let me tell you all about it."

We took a seat and waited for him to begin. I could see he was nervous as he wrung his hands and wiped them down both pants legs in a sort of repeating pattern. Funny how I picked up on little things like that.

"I hired Susan a few weeks after you two were born. One baby would have been hard enough, so I hired Susan to come in a few hours a day to help out. Susan ended up moving in as a full time nanny. Susan and I became great friends through the years as we raised you two boys. The first few years of her being there was strictly a professional relationship. She worked for me and I paid her every week to help me take care of you. I don't know exactly when things changed, but they did. We both began developing feelings that were hard to explain."

We listened silently as Uncle Charles talked. I was very proud as told us things he had probably never told anybody.

"It wasn't long after that Susan found out I was different. That is a whole other story for another time. But, it resulted in her moving out of the house. She was so freaked out about it that she wouldn't even let me explain. Our relationship was so new I thought she would never speak to me again. After a few days she finally agreed to sit down and talk to me about it. I

218

don't know if it was her love for me, or the love she had for you two boys that brought her to the house that day. But I laid everything I knew about werewolves on the table that day in hopes that I wouldn't lose her forever."

"So you're dating Susan, the babysitter?" Matt asked.

"Yes," Uncle Charles said as he continued his story. "I don't think she was ok with the whole werewolf thing, but she seemed to accept it. She wouldn't move back in the house, but our relationship continued to grow again. And, she was there nearly every day helping me with you two. As you got older, she didn't need to be there as much. But we continued seeing each other and have all these years,"

"So, if she knows about us, why did you make us leave? I would have liked to see her and get to know the woman that helped raise me," said Matt.

I definitely was not expecting the response Matt gave. But it definitely made perfect sense.

"She knows about werewolves, but that's all she knows. She freaked so bad when she found out about me that I have been too scared to tell her about anything else. I would have loved for you to meet her sooner. But, I didn't want you to think I was trying to replace your mother," said Uncle Charles.

"Dad, I never even met Mom. I don't remember a single thing about her. The only woman I knew growing up was Susan. Why would you take that away from us?" Matt asked.

"Matt, I can't even begin to tell you about all the mistakes I have made as a father. One day you will know what it is like. You will make bad calls as you do your absolute best at raising your children and being a dad," said Uncle Charles sadly.

"Uncle Charles, you were an AWESOME dad!" I said even though he wasn't technically my dad at all. But, he was the only one I ever knew.

"Thanks, Luke. That means a lot. I love you boys, and I have always tried to do what was best for you."

"I love you too Dad. But, when are we going to get to meet Susan?" Matt asked.

"Well, after you guys left last night, I really did some thinking. I don't want to hide anything from her anymore. I brought her here this weekend to meet the family. I am going to tell her everything. And, I am going to propose," said Uncle Charles proudly.

"You're getting married?" asked Matt excitedly.

"Yes, Matt. I guess I am," Uncle Charles replied.

18

I had noticed that shortly after we came in to talk to Uncle Charles, the familiar strange feeling appeared in my chest. I figured the man from the council had probably arrived. Almost as soon as Uncle Charles had finished his story the feeling disappeared. I became nervous about what was going on.

I blew the feeling off once again thinking maybe I hadn't completely figured them out yet. I had decided the feelings were to warn me when evil was near. But, since I had started having random flashes of the feelings, I wasn't so sure. I thought I was gaining a new ability, but now, I wondered if it was an ability at all.

For some reason an idea sort of popped in my head. Something had sparked a memory from just yesterday. I couldn't believe I hadn't already thought about it. Once we were finished congratulating Uncle Charles, I remembered I had business to take care of. I excused myself and pulled my cell phone out on the way out.

I sent Walter a quick message. "How long before more Travelports will be ready?"

A few seconds later a response chimed. It said, "I have four machines in production as we speak. They will probably be ready in twenty-four to forty-eight hours."

"I need them ASAP! Send them to me as soon as they are ready," I send back.

A plan was forming in my head for rescuing my mom. I wasn't completely sure it would work, but it was worth a try. The major component of my plan involved all of the soldiers being able to go at the same time via Travelport of course.

"Will do! I think you will be more than pleased with this new batch," read the response from Walter.

Another forty-eight hours before I would be able to see if my plan worked. I met Ava at the top of the stairs on the way to my room.

"Hi! I was just on my way to find you," she said smiling.

"So was I!" I said.

"What you doing?" she asked in a rather happy tone.

"Well, I have an idea I may need your help with. I think we are going to need some spells," I said.

I began telling her all about the plan to rescue my mother. I went step by step the way I saw it playing out. Each time I mentioned a spell we might need she pulled one from her pocket and put it in my hand, giggling each time.

"Already done! That's what I've been doing all day. It's really scary how much we think alike sometimes," she said.

Well, it was settled, I thought to myself. As soon as Walter got us the Travelports, we would be ready to fly!

Ava and I decided to go to the theater downstairs for a movie. Neither of us could think of anything better to do. When we got to the bottom of the stairs we met Uncle Charles and Susan.

"Hey guys, where are you off to in such a hurry?" Uncle Charles asked us.

"We were going to watch a movie. You should join us." I said.

"What do you think?" Uncle Charles asked Susan.

"Sounds like fun!" said Susan.

I could hear Susan's heart beating faster and faster. I couldn't tell if she was excited or scared. It was probably more of the latter though.

"Are they werewolves too?" whispered Susan as they followed us toward the theater.

"Not exactly," whispered Uncle Charles.

I glanced back just enough to see Uncle Charles's face blush red with embarrassment. I smiled knowing he was aware that I could hear everything they were saying.

We let Susan pick the movie we were going to watch. We found it quite ironic when she decided on *Dracula* as her movie of choice. She went on and on about how much she loved the movie and that it was her favorite one of all time. I was actually kind of excited about watching the movie again. It was the first time I had watched it since I found out vampires actually exist.

"How many have I met so far?" whispered Susan after the movie had been on several minutes.

"Babe, there is so much more to it than who is and who isn't a werewolf," whispered Uncle Charles.

For a minute I thought Uncle Charles was going to tell her about everything during the movie. Instead, Susan focused her attention back on the movie, and they were quiet for several minutes. My phone vibrated and I pulled it out of my pocket.

"Dude, where are you guys?" said the message I received from Matt.

"Ava and I are in the theater with your Dad and Susan. Come watch Dracula with us!" I replied back.

It wasn't long before Matt and Jenna came in and took a seat with the rest of us. I hoped Matt wasn't mad that we hadn't invited him to watch with us in the first place. All I needed was for him to attack me again. That would really freak Susan out.

"Is Matt or his friend a werewolf?" Susan asked.

"Yes, they are both werewolves," replied Uncle Charles.

They whispered so quietly I was certain that the only person overhearing their conversation was me.

"What about Luke and Ava?" Susan asked.

"No. They are not werewolves," said Uncle Charles.

I could tell Uncle Charles was getting irritated by her asking about how was a werewolf. He dodged the bullet nicely when she had asked about Ava and me. I couldn't believe how persistent she was.

They were quiet for the remainder of the movie. I was on edge anticipating the questions that would come next. I would not have been any help in coming up with a way for Uncle Charles to tell Susan about the whole supernatural community.

Once the credits started rolling, Ava got up and turned on the lights. Everyone else began standing up and stretching from sitting so long.

"There must not be any vampire movie writers. Vampires in the movies are nothing like the ones today. Right, Luke?" asked Ava as she rejoined the group.

A chill ran down my spine just as my heart suddenly dropped to my stomach. The room fell silent as we anticipated a horrific reaction from Susan.

"Did she say what I think she just said?" Susan asked Uncle Charles.

It was a little more than a whisper this time. I knew everyone else in the room could hear this time.

"Yes," Uncle Charles said quietly. "Susan, I…" was all he got out before Susan cut him off.

"Charles! Is there something you would like to tell me?" Susan asked.

"Susan, I love you with all my heart. But there is so much more than just werewolves in the world," Uncle Charles said nervously.

"So vampires are real too?" Susan asked.

"Yes they are," said Uncle Charles.

"And so are Faeries, and elves, and…" said Matt

"And trolls!" Jenna exclaimed.

"Don't forget about me! You can't leave out witches! And why did nobody think to tell me one of us doesn't know about the supernatural folk?" Ava asked.

My face turned hot and I knew I was blushing. I couldn't believe I had forgotten to tell Ava about Susan.

"Vampires are really real?" Susan asked.

Uncle Charles looked at me and I knew he wanted me to be the one to tell her. Instead of telling her, I decided to show her. Time to make it or break it. Either she would accept us, or she would run for the hills screaming.

Using my vampire speed I ran around the group and stopped right beside Susan. She continued to look at the spot where I had disappeared right before her eyes. I cleared my throat quietly so she would look my way. I noticed the color begin to drain from her face a little and feared the worst.

"Susan, you helped raise me all these years. And you have been with Dad even after you found out about us. What are you so scared of?" asked Matt.

"Matt, I always knew something was different about you. I always wondered about the noises you made while you were sleeping. It almost sounded like little howls," Susan said. "I have never been scared by any of you. I wasn't even scared the night I watched your father shift for the first time."

"The first time?" asked Uncle Charles.

"I have watched you shift in your sleep more times than I care to remember, Charles," said Susan giggling. "Didn't you ever wonder why I disappeared from the bed some nights?"

"I guess I never thought about it," said Uncle Charles as his face blushed with embarrassment.

It was the second time that night that Uncle Charles had been embarrassed. It was the only two times I had ever seen him that way in all the years I had been with him.

"I was scared the first time I saw you Charles, but I got over it. You should know that since I came back to you. I haven't been scared at all. I feel safe with you. What I have been is disappointed. I am disappointed that it took somebody else to bring up the rest of the supernatural world," Susan said.

"Susan, I am so sorry. I have wanted to tell you so many times, but I was scared I would lose you forever," Uncle Charles said.

"Keeping secrets is the quickest way to lose me, Charles," Susan told him.

"You never have to worry about that again," said Uncle Charles.

I knew a huge weight had been lifted. I couldn't imagine having to keep who and what I was a complete secret from the person I loved. I honestly didn't think I would be able to do it.

"Well, now that we got that out of the way," said Matt smiling.

Matt's happiness showed on his face. I didn't know what Jenna had said to him, but it completely changed Matt's attitude toward Susan. I guessed he was happy to finally have a mother figure in his life.

"So, what do you want to do this evening?" Ava asked me quietly.

I took this to mean she would like to have some us time. I definitely wasn't opposed to the idea.

"Would you like to go out?" I asked her.

I had no idea where to take her, but I didn't really care where we went. I decided to let her choose.

"We could grab something to eat and go to a movie," she said.

I remembered clearly the last trip we had made to the movies. We had been introduced to the green eyed vamps that night. If that was where we were going I hoped it didn't end the way it had that night.

"That sounds great!" I told her.

Ava wanted to freshen up and change before we left, so I decided to do the same. As soon as I jumped in the shower the strange feeling in my chest started up again. I quickly finished my shower in vampire speed and dressed just as quickly. I was determined to find out who, or what, was causing the feeling. Unfortunately, the feeling stopped just as fast as it started.

I finished getting ready at a normal pace. When I went to get my watch and necklace off the dresser I was stopped dead in my tracks. My watch was on my dresser right where I left it. But, to my surprise, my necklace was not! I searched my entire room in seconds. I didn't miss a single corner or crevice. Not that it could have just randomly fallen off the dresser anyway.

I burst from my room heading straight to find Grandpa. Somebody would be in trouble for taking my stuff. I knocked on Matt's door across the hall but nobody answered. Next I knocked on Ava's door. Rachel answered the door.

"Was Ava just in my room?" I blurted out as soon as the door opened.

"Ava is in the shower, Luke. Is something wrong?" she asked.

I knew she could see I was upset about something.

"Somebody was just in my room. My necklace is gone!" I exclaimed.

"Oh, my!" Rachel said.

I rushed downstairs from there to look for Grandpa. I was lucky and found him in his office which was the first place I looked.

"Grandpa!" I shouted as soon as I made it in the door.

"Luke, what's wrong? Why are you shouting?" Grandpa asked.

"Somebody was just in my room! They took my necklace! We have to find it!" I continued to shout.

I was growing more afraid by the second. My necklace was the only thing that kept me alive on two different occasions.

I didn't want to be without it while the dark elf was still on the loose.

"Luke, please calm down. I promise we will get to the bottom of this," Grandpa said as he picked up his phone from the desk.

"I want every person and every square inch of this mansion searched immediately. Someone has stolen Luke's necklace and I want it found NOW!" Grandpa growled into his phone.

He didn't wait for a response before he hung up and immediately dialed another number. He repeated the part about someone stealing my necklace. Only this time he told the person he was talking to he wanted the security feed checked in my room. He hung up quickly.

I nearly forgot all about the problem at hand as I became concerned about them having a security feed in my room. That meant they could spy on me anytime they wanted. I would have to deal with that later, I thought to myself. We had more pressing issues at hand.

"We need to go to headquarters. The cameras should have picked up the thief," said Grandpa.

We both stormed out of the office and in a few minutes were walking up to the security booth. The man behind the monitors watched the images from my bedroom closely. It was really quite disturbing.

"It happened within the last 20 minutes. Run it up to when I went into the bathroom to take a shower. That's when it happened," I told the man.

I watched as the image sped up. He slowed it down once I came in the room and headed for the shower. A few seconds later my blood went cold and a shiver ran down my whole body as I watched the monitor. I was horrified as we saw the dark elf appear standing right in front of the dresser where my necklace was sitting. He quickly reached out and grabbed it. Suddenly, his head turned directly toward the camera. I was shocked to watch him hold the necklace up and smile revealing his horrid sharp pointy teeth. I didn't know how such an evil creature could smile about anything.

Just like the feeling in my chest earlier, the dark elf disappeared. Grandpa pulled out his phone and made a call.

"Call off the search. We found out who it was," Grandpa said. He was silent as the other person responded.

"Bring it to me immediately!" Grandpa ordered into the phone.

When he hung up the phone he again dialed another number.

"I need you to come to headquarters, now!" he said.

A few seconds later, Uncle Charles exited the elevator and came over to us. I noticed he was holding a small object in his hand.

"What is it?" I asked.

"I don't know, but she will," Grandpa said pointing toward Rachel as she exited the elevator. I was happy to see Ava right behind her.

"Luke, are you alright?" Ava asked as she ran past her mother and hugged me tight. "What's going on?"

I repeated to her about my necklace being stolen. I didn't get the part about who stole it out before Rachel joined the group. I stopped talking and watched as Uncle Charles handed the weird little object to Rachel.

"Where did this come from?" asked Rachel. I could hear in her voice that she was quite angry.

"We found it stuck underneath the table in the great room. We don't know how it got there," said Uncle Charles.

"I think I found something," said the man working the booth. "Watch this."

The scene on the monitor was instantly familiar to me. It was when Grandpa and I had been in there talking to the man from the council. We watched as the camera zoomed in on the man. More particularly it zoomed on the arm he was holding under the table as we talked. We were shocked to see him reach into his pocket and pull out the strange object and put it under the table. When he pulled his arm back out, the object was gone.

"This is a spell," Rachel said drawing our attention back to her. "That man put a spell in the mansion. The worst part is, that this kind of spell is created to allow any being to warp anywhere this is placed.

"That explains how the dark elf got in my room! They are working together!" I shouted.

"What?" Ava asked in a rather shaky voice.

I quickly explained about the dark elf appearing in my room and how he took the necklace. Ava, Uncle Charles, and Rachel's mouths hung open wide in shock as I told the story.

"I want a complete search run on that man!" Grandpa ordered the man behind the monitors. "I want to know everything about him!"

"I'll get right on it," said the man as he quickly got to work.

I was quiet for several minutes as everyone else talked about it being an outrage that the mansion had been infiltrated.

"I can't find anything on him. The council says he has never worked for them," said the man.

I couldn't believe what I was hearing. My home had been invaded twice in the past week. Actually, I remembered the feeling a couple other times. There was no telling how many times one of the two of them had been spying on us without anyone even knowing.

"This is an outrage!" Grandpa exclaimed. "How do two different invasions happen without a single person noticing?"

"Both times I was injured, the same venom showed up in the wounds. The first time was the dark elf's arrow. The second time was directly from the source when we followed that weird coach into a cave full of the most awful creatures you will ever meet," I said as I tried to put the pieces of the puzzle together.

"So how does the guy we thought was from the council fit in?" asked Grandpa.

"That's the only piece I can't seem to fit," I replied.

"What if the coach and the man from the council, or not from the council, or whoever he is, is actually the same person," Ava said.

"How is that possible? They don't even look alike!" I said.

"What if it's a shifter," said Rachel.

"I don't think it's a coincidence that the weird coach disappeared the same day the man from the council showed up here," said Ava.

"You might be on to something, Ava," said Grandpa.

"The question is who is it?" I said.

"Only one person comes to mind that is powerful enough to pull this off," said Uncle Charles.

I knew who Uncle Charles was referring to before he even said the name. I was horrified to figure out that Nhados was behind everything. He would pay if I could ever get the chance to face him.

19

Our group dispersed as everyone had a lot to think about. The question that kept coming to mind was why did the dark elf take the necklace instead of just attacking? He obviously knew the necklace was protecting me. Why else would he come and take it? It occurred to me that maybe the dark elf was taunting me the way he looked and smiled at the camera.

Just as Ava and I got on the elevator my vision went black. It started the same as all the times before with Nhados holding the baby, and Nhados standing next to the toddler aged little boy. This time, the vision flashed to a new scene. This time, the boy standing next to Nhados appeared to be around seven or eight years old.

When I came to I was surprised to realize I was still on my feet. Every other time I had a vision I had crashed to the floor. Maybe my power of visions was evolving again. I definitely liked not waking up on the floor.

"What just happened?" Ava asked.

"Another vision," I replied.

I was still a little woozy from the vision. I was still curious about the not falling down part of it.

"What did you see, Luke?" asked Ava.

"Same as before, but, after the toddler there was a kid," I said.

"You still don't know what it could mean?"

"No, I don't have a clue!" I said.

I was completely stumped when it came to the visions I had been having lately. I couldn't imagine Nhados having a child. Who would want to have a baby with such a horrible being? And, if the baby isn't his, whose is it? These were the questions that kept running through my head.

"We aren't even safe here at the mansion anymore," I told Ava once we were headed upstairs in the elevator.

"Luke, Mom is going to destroy the talisman. The dark one can't come back here. The most powerful of magic guards these grounds. And if I know Mr. Carrington, nobody will get in here so easily again," Ava said trying to comfort me.

I knew we were as safe as possible. Ava's words actually helped me to calm down so I could think more clearly.

"I'm guessing we aren't going out," said Ava.

"I really don't think it's a good idea. The dark one is out there and he has the only thing that can keep me alive," I told her.

"I know, Luke. I was just really looking forward to going out somewhere with you. We haven't been on a real date since we were in England. And your mom was with us for that one," Ava explained.

"I'm sorry, Ava. I promise when things settle down I will make it up to you."

"You better," she said as she gave me an evil sort of grin.

I leaned down and kissed her gently. I knew what she meant. I had worked so hard to come home and live a normal sort of life, but something always came up. I wondered if Ava and I would ever be able to have a normal life. I needed to clear my mind. There was only one thing I knew of that could help do that.

"Will you go run with me?" I asked Ava.

I knew we would be just as safe outside as we were in the mansion. As long as we stayed inside the stone walls of the property that is.

"I would love to, Luke," Ava said.

We ran for the rest of the night. Ava had to use her transformation spell twice. I think we covered every square inch of the property. I think we were both pretty much exhausted when we made it up to my room. I climbed up on my bed and Ava climbed up beside me. We were both content just lying there holding each other. In a matter of minutes I drifted off to sleep. I'm not sure how long we were asleep before Ava's phone started blaring and someone was knocking on my door.

"Ava Hadison! You get yourself out here right now!" shouted Ava's mom as soon as the door was opened a crack.

"Mom! Please stop yelling. You're going to wake up the whole mansion," said Ava as she hurried out the door.

"Good! I want everybody to know you are in big trouble young lady!" Rachel shouted. I think she got louder after Ava seemed to give her the idea.

"MOM, PLEASE!" Ava pleaded. "I'm sorry. We fell asleep."

"I was worried sick about you, Ava. I have been texting you for hours. You are too young to be doing this sort of thing," Rachel said as she pointed from me to my room and back to me.

I was worried Ava would be grounded for eternity. Rachel was madder than I had ever seen her.

"Mom, we didn't even make out tonight. It's not what you think," Ava continued to plead our case.

"You just march yourself straight to bed! I'll deal with you later. And as for you," Rachel said putting her finger in the center of my chest, "I'll be letting your mother know about this," Rachel said glaring at me.

Wow! I thought to myself as I watched them walk to their room and go in. I was a little upset by what Rachel was implying. Ava and I had never done anything but kiss in the years we had been dating. I hadn't even tried to take it to second base yet, and I really didn't have any plans to anytime soon.

I climbed back in the bed not expecting to be able to fall asleep after all the drama that had just happened. When I finally did, the same familiar dream started. Nhados was first with the baby, then the toddler, and again, the young kid. But, this time it changed again. This time there was another kid. He looked to be around twelve or thirteen years old. For the first time I saw the resemblance between the different aged boys. I came to the

238

conclusion that they were all the same boy. What I still couldn't figure out is what the vision meant.

I woke up the next morning to the sound of my phone going off. I reached over to the night stand to answer it.

"Hello?" I said groggily. This had better be important. I thought to myself.

"Luke! I have a surprise for you! Come outside!" said Walter's voice on the other end.

"What?" I said not completely awake and alert yet.

"I need you to wake up and come outside! I have a huge surprise!" Walter said excitedly.

"I'll be there in a minute," I said as I hung up the phone.

I suddenly comprehended what was going on. I jumped out of the bed and threw on some clothes quickly. I was down the stairs and outside in seconds.

"Wow that was fast!" Walter exclaimed.

He met me on the front steps smiling happily. I immediately saw what he was so happy about. Sitting in the driveway was two new and improved Travelports. The machines were similar to the first one in color and shape, but they were noticeably bigger. They were at least twice the size of the two seated model.

"Those are awesome!" I told him.

"Thanks! I'm glad you like them. They are big enough to carry your whole team. I did one for you, and one for the

England team. I was going to deliver it there, but I was told the team was here in Little Rock," Walter explained.

"They are!" I exclaimed. "I'm glad you brought them both here. We are going to test them out as soon as everyone is ready to leave."

I pulled out my cell phone and sent a mass message to all of the soldiers. I told both teams to meet me at headquarters dressed for battle.

"We need somebody to take us home," said Walter.

"Come with me. You can take the Travelport I have and we can pick it up later. I have something I have to do right now. You should really consider moving here to the mansion. I can have you a top of the line lab right here at the mansion. And what's even better, you will be protected by me, the soldiers, and the entire Little Rock pack of wolves," I told him as we walked through the front doors.

I headed straight for the elevator. I was ready for the soldiers to leave as soon as possible for this mission.

"Welcome to headquarters, Walter," I said as we exited the elevator.

I glanced over and noticed Walter's eyes had grown quite large as he took in the sights from the massive main room. I was surprised when he headed straight for the security booth. I guess he decided to take over the quick tour I had planned for him while I waited for the soldiers to get there.

Walter introduced himself to the man working the security booth. They immediately began talking about the top of the line security system. I took the time to go to the vault and grab my sword so I would be ready when everyone else arrived. I returned to the security booth in my white uniform with the Koichi sword secured in its place on my back.

"What do you think, Walter?"

"I think I can help you with your security, Luke. I worked as a security engineer for the government for several years. I can share a few tips and tricks I learned along the way," said Walter.

"I meant what do you think about moving to the mansion? We could really use you here. I have some ideas I want you to work on," I told him.

"I don't think I could move here. I have a family back home. I can't just up and leave them," Walter said.

"I would never want you to leave your family, Walter. You can bring them with you," I told him. "They would be safe here."

"What will your pack say about having a bunch of demons in their house?" Walter asked.

"Demons? I don't understand," I said confused.

"You didn't actually think Alexander would have a bunch of humans working for him did you?

Just about that time the elevators opened drawing my attention to the new arrivals. Grandpa and Uncle Charles walked across the floor toward us. I had added both of them to the list of people I sent my message to.

"What's going on, Luke? It's great to see you again, Walter," Grandpa said shaking Walter's hand and then looking over to me for an explanation.

I explained about the new Travelport machines. I quickly told them my plans to try and rescue Mom. I watched looks of fear spread across both their faces as I explained.

Just then the soldiers began to arrive. They headed toward the dressing room to get ready seeing me already dressed and ready. They already knew what time it was.

"Shouldn't we wait for Dakota before rushing to face the dark one?" asked Matt walking up to us on his way to the dressing room.

"Actually, I have a plan for that too!" I said looking from Walter to Grandpa.

It took them a few seconds to realize what I was implying. Faster than Walter and my Grandpa could see, I was suddenly standing there holding a vial of the daylight serum.

"What do you think?" I asked.

"Well, Luke, are you ready for the serum to go public?" Grandpa asked.

"If you are going to use the serum, Dakota would be the absolute best choice," said Matt.

"You realize this will change everything!" exclaimed Walter.

I knew the consequences for letting the serum's existence became known. If Dakota started walking around in the daylight people would ask questions.

"Should we vote?" I asked. "All in favor of Dakota being with us all the time," I said raising my hand in the air.

I looked around the crowd that had suddenly formed surrounding us. The original five soldiers were the first to raise their hands. They realized the importance of having Dakota around all the time. The rest of the soldiers followed suit next. We all turned to the adults in the room. Uncle Charles and Walter slowly raised their hands.

"I guess the decision is made," said Grandpa.

I was happy as I watched him raise his hand as well. I rushed to Dakota's room at vampire speed. It took some time, but I was finally able to wake him up.

"What's going on, man?" asked Dakota groggily.

"This is going to be the best day of your life!" I told Dakota as I showed him the vial of daylight serum.

I explained what it was and that it would allow him to go out in the sunlight. His eyes got big with this news. I added how the whole team voted for him to be with us all the time. I don't think there was any question about whether he wanted to do it. He quickly drank the serum as soon as I handed it to him. I watched as he closed his eyes and raised his face to the sky. When he opened his eyes again I noticed they were clear from the redness from being woke up so early in the day.

Dakota jumped out of his coffin landing on his feet standing right in front of me. I quickly went over the plans to rescue my mother before we both bolted out the door heading for headquarters.

When we got there I realized Walter was gone. The Travelport was also missing from where I had parked it. I knew he had already headed home.

"Walter said he would talk to you in a few days. He said he was going to talk to his family about your offer," said Grandpa.

"I hope you know what you're getting yourself into," said Uncle Charles.

"I don't think we really have a choice. Do you really think an elf is any match for the power we have right here?" I asked motioning toward the eight soldiers standing behind me,"

"Just be careful, Luke. And don't underestimate him," said Grandpa.

"You know we will, Grandpa!" I said.

I would never want any of my soldiers to get hurt. I considered them my extended family and closest friends.

"Let's do this!" Jenna said.

I knew she was as ready as I was to get our parents back. I turned to the man at the booth and asked him about communication for everyone. He pulled out watches and handed each of us one. Next were the familiar earpieces. We all inserted them after attaching the watches to our arms.

I led the way to the large elevator at the end of the room. I knew all of us would never fit in the small one. We were headed outside, anyway. I explained to Eric and his crew about how the Travelport worked on our way up the elevator. It was really easy, so it didn't take long for him to be up to speed.

We all climbed in the Travelports. Matt and I sat in the front of our machine. Ava, Jenna, and Dakota sat in the seat behind us. That left two seats in the very back empty. That would be plenty of room to bring Mom and Dante home.

"Just touch the screen," I said to Eric and his team through our communication devices. "Take us to my mother," I said once I heard the now familiar voice ask for our destination. I heard Eric say take us to Luke's mother over in his own Travelport.

The windows of both Travelports began to slide closed as the machines lifted off the ground into the sky. Once we were above the trees we shot forward. To my surprise we almost instantly slowed down and started going down. I looked around and realized we were in Little Rock. We were out in the industrial district of the city. I noticed large warehouses all around. Most of them looked as if they weren't being used anymore.

The Travelports touched down outside one of the larger buildings and we all jumped out once the windows were opened.

"They must be inside," I said as I began walking toward one of the doors leading inside the building.

"Wait!" Ava said. "Everyone take one of these."

She handed out a small round orb filled with black smoke to all of the soldiers. I knew my team was familiar with Ava's spells, but I doubted the new ones had.

"They are spells," I said seeing the confused looks on their faces.

"They aren't just any spells. Whoever gets close to the dark one first needs to hit him with one of these. It will take away his power to jump. He want be able to escape," Ava said happily.

"Are we ready?" I asked the group.

"As ready as we can be," said Eric.

"Everybody watch out for those arrows. They have a nasty bite!" I told everybody.

The soldiers prepared themselves and I continued toward the warehouse. It was finally time to confront the dark elf. And this time he wouldn't get a lucky shot on me like he did last time. I had my team with me and he didn't stand a chance.

We walked into the warehouse to find out that it was just a huge open room. A few catwalks were running the length of the building up in the rafters of the roof. I didn't take much time looking around the building once I spotted what was hanging from the rafters in the middle of the huge empty floor. I immediately realized two of the four people hanging were Mom and Dante. I was completely shocked to find that Jack and Cameron were the other two. I suddenly felt horrible not even knowing they had been taken again. What kind of friend was I? They hung from their wrists high over their heads by heavy chains running up into the rafters.

I noticed Dakota already had his bow ready with an arrow locked in place. I drew my sword once I noticed my family and friends hanging high in the air. I quickened my pace but someone grabbed my arm stopping me in my tracks.

"Not so fast, Luke, you need to be completely focused. Focus your senses on every inch of this room," Dakota whispered to me.

I stopped and tried to focus all of my senses on my surroundings. I immediately realized the dark one was in the room. I could smell him from the mission I completed as a wolf. I had studied his scent so I would never forget it, and I hadn't. I could hear rats squeaking at the other end of the warehouse. I could hear cockroaches and other crawling insects scurrying about all over the building. All of a sudden I heard the pop of a bow. My hearing drew my attention to the sound and just in time I saw the arrow flying and sliced it out of the air with my sword.

"Your fast half breed!" said the voice of the dark elf. I had only heard him speak once, but it was an evil hissing voice that you couldn't forget.

"But you can't hit what you can't see," said the voice.

I noticed Dakota drew back his bow and was aiming it toward the place where the voice last came.

"Ahh, a fellow archer!" said the voice from the other side of the building. "It is very curious that a vampire would be out here in the daylight. Let's see how good you are."

Suddenly there was another pop sound from the dark one's bow. I quickly spotted the arrow coming my way and prepared to slice it away like I had the last one. Instead, I heard the sound of metal hitting metal and the arrow flew off course. Dakota had shot the arrow right out of the air.

A bright blue light shot out from beside me toward the previous location of the voice. I knew instantly that it was Jenna with her electricity power. She hit the catwalk electrifying the entire platform. A screeching sound came from the far end of the platform.

"Wow! This is going to be fun!" said the dark elf's voice back on the other side of the building. "A half-breed, a vampire archer, and a weird shocking werewolf, you are just full of surprises."

"You have no idea!" I shouted.

I was beginning to get angry with him calling me a half breed. I jumped into the air at vampire speed slicing through the air where the voice came from. I felt the sword make contact without even having to look at the blood dripping from my blade.

"You are going to pay for that!" said the dark elf. I could smell the blood coming from the wound I had inflicted on the dark one.

Apparently I wasn't the only one because suddenly the dark elf shrieked again as there was a puff of black smoke. Jordan had gotten him with one of Ava's spells.

"What did you do to me?" shouted the dark elf.

When the smoke cleared the dark elf stood there facing us from the catwalk. Suddenly, Patrick appeared on the catwalk right next to the dark elf. He kicked his foot out quickly catching the dark one's arm holding the bow. We watched as the bow flew out of his hand and crashed to the concrete floor below. The dark elf pulled an arrow out of the quiver on his back and stabbed it in Patrick's outstretched leg. He crumbled to the catwalk in pain.

The next thing we saw was Matt take off running down the middle of the room. He jumped into the air instantly transforming into the huge dragon. He beat his gigantic wings and turned his head toward the dark elf. I knew what Matt planned to do next as I watched him inhale deeply. Apparently the dark one knew what was coming as well because he started sprinting down the catwalk at a supernatural speed. He just barely got out of the way before Matt blew a continuous blast of fire from his mouth. He continued to blow fire as he tried to catch the elf with it.

We watched as the dark elf grabbed the hand rail and jumped over the side. He fell gracefully to the floor landing on both feet. He stood up slowly as he raised his face to look down the length of the room at us. He gave us an evil grin like the one he flashed in the security video.

"Why don't you face me like a man, Luke? What are you so scared of?" the elf asked me.

I watched as the elf pulled something from his waist. He held it out to his side with one hand and two long blades shot out in opposite directions.

"He is defenseless now. Right?" I asked

"Luke don't do this," said Ava.

"What other choice do we have? Somebody has to take him down," I said.

I knew she didn't want me to against him, but somebody had to.

"You're going to need this," Jenna said as she threw her sword to me.

I caught the sword in mid-air. I looked down at the two blades I held in my hands. It was going to be me or him. I hoped one of the blades would soon be sticking out of his chest.

"Watch both blades, Luke," Dakota said.

I took off at vampire speed. The elf apparently sprinted toward me as well. We met almost directly below my friends and family hanging from the rafters in the middle of the floor. Our motions were probably faster that anyone in the room could even see as he cut and sliced with his double bladed weapon. I easily blocked every blow.

The dark elf tried to cut and stab me for several minutes before I could tell that he was slowing down. A few more minutes and he would be tired out and I would have him. All of a sudden there was a puff of purple smoke. The smoke engulfed the elf to the point I could no longer see him. Just before I could back up his weapon shot out of the smoke and stabbed me right in the middle of the top part of my leg. Just as quickly as it went in, the dark elf pulled it back out. I looked down and realized the wound was already healing. It was good to know it wasn't coated with whatever his arrows were.

"Oops, wrong one!" Ava said once the smoke cleared and she realized it hadn't phased the dark elf.

Suddenly there was another puff of purple smoke. I noticed the color was much darker this time. It was so dark it was nearly black. We immediately heard the dark elf shriek with anger.

"Let me go you stupid witch!" The elf shouted and hissed.

I walked over to the dark elf lying on the ground. He was wrapped in the familiar silver net and unable to move. I put the tip of my sword on his throat and slowly began pushing it forward to get my point across.

"If you want to leave this building alive I advise you to keep your mouth shut. And you definitely don't want to talk to my girlfriend like that ever again," I said to the now helpless dark elf.

I didn't wait for a response as I forgot about him and turned my attention to how I would get my loved ones down from the roof.

"Help me," I told the guys. "I need you to catch them."

I jumped into the air and sliced my sword through the chain holding my mother first. Her body dropped toward the floor and I watched Matt and Eric catch her gracefully and lower her gently to the floor. I cut down the other three before I rushed to my mother's side. The guys had already untied her hands. I quickly reached to her neck to check if she had a pulse.

"They are still alive," said the dark elf. "They will wake up eventually."

"You better not have hurt them," I snarled at the elf.

I hadn't noticed before, but I looked down and realized Mom was wearing my necklace. I let her keep wearing it. Maybe it would protect her like it had me.

"We need to get them home," said Ava. "I'll call Dr. Blevins, but we need to move! I don't think we can trust what he says," Ava said pointing at our prisoner.

We all picked up the unconscious people and started carrying them toward the Travelports.

"Stay with him," I told Jordan and Katie.

I didn't think he could escape the spell, but I wasn't going to take any chances. Just as we made our way out to the parking lot, several black vehicles came to a screeching halt close to the Travelports. I wasn't surprised to see Grandpa get out of the first vehicle. We didn't slow down as we continued carrying our parents and friends and loaded them into the machines.

Once they were loaded I turned to see that Jordan and Katie were dragging the dark one by his feet out the door to the warehouse toward us.

"Where do you want him?" asked Katie.

"You let him live?" asked Grandpa. The way he said it sounded like he was angry that I hadn't killed the elf.

"It's not for us to decide who lives or dies, Grandpa. The council will decide his fate," I said.

"Right," Grandpa said sarcastically.

"I'm going to take Mom home. Do whatever you want with him," I said.

I wanted Grandpa to know I was upset about what he was implying. Why would he want me to choose to take someone else's life? It wasn't for us to decide. Was that not why members were elected into the council?

"Let's go, guys," I said to my soldiers.

Everyone immediately loaded into the Travelports. When the voice asked us for our destination I was happy to finally be able to tell her, take us home.

20

We were home in seconds. I pulled the Travelport into the elevator. It barely fit, but it did fit. The window opened as we were being lowered into headquarters. As soon as I had the Travelport parked I grabbed my mother up and jumped down to the floor. I quickly carried her into the hospital wing where Dr. Blevins waited with four empty beds.

Just as I lay Mom down on the bed I heard her say my name softly. I was so happy I nearly started crying. I watched as she started to wake up and look around the room.

"What happened? Where am I?" She asked as Dante, Jack, and Cam were brought in and placed on the beds.

"I think they are going to be alright. Everybody is starting to wake up," said Dr. Blevins.

Mom must have been feeling ok because she sat up and swung her legs over the side of the bed.

"Take it easy, Mom!" I told her.

"I'm ok, baby. Just tell me what happened. The last think I remember is saying my vows and then somebody grabbed my arm. After that everything is a blank," Mom said.

I explained everything that happened with them being abducted, up through the final battle with the dark elf.

"I've been out for a week?" was all Mom managed to say. I could tell she was sort of in shock by what I had told her.

Mom stood up and walked over to Dante who was just starting to sit up. I watched as Mom helped him up and held him steady while he cleared his head from whatever the elf had done to them. I walked over to Cam and helped him up and noticed Ava was doing the same as Jack when my vision suddenly went black.

The familiar vision with Nhados and the children came into focus. The infant, toddler, young boy, and then the teenager played in my mind. I woke up realizing it was exactly same as before. Something else that hadn't changed was the fact that I was on my feet again for the second time.

"Did you have another vision?" Ava asked as she put her hand on my shoulder.

"Yes. And, it's exactly the same as the last one," I replied.

"Tell me what you saw," said Mom walking over to my side.

I explained all about the visions I had been having. She didn't have any more of a clue than we did about what the visions meant.

"I want to run some blood tests, but I think everyone will be fine," Dr. Blevins said bringing needles and tubes to Cam's bed.

"Oh, I hate needles," said Cam.

"So how did the dark elf get you two again?" I asked Cam trying to take his mind off what Dr. Blevins was doing with his arm.

"Dad and I were coming to see you the other night. I don't remember what room we jumped to but the dark one was there already. He grabbed us both and that was the last thing I remember," Cam explained.

"I am so sorry, buddy," I told him.

"It wasn't your fault, Luke. What are you sorry about?"

"I'm sorry I wasn't a better friend. I'm sorry I didn't even realize the two of you were gone," I said.

"Luke, you are a great friend!" Cam said as he jumped off the bed and into my arms.

He hugged me tight and I was glad none of my family or friends had been hurt by that horrible creature.

"Luke, you can't blame yourself for everything all the time," said Jack. "You and your team do far more than anybody should ever expect from you," said Jack.

I lowered Cam to the floor and turned to Jack.

"We should have been more careful. I knew my brother would stop at nothing to get Cam and I back after Jordan rescued us," Jack said.

"What? The dark one is your brother?" I asked.

"He wasn't always like that. Shawn used to be the nicest man you would ever meet. It was an honor to call him my brother," said Jack.

"So what happened to him? Why did he turn evil?" Ava asked.

"Many years ago, there was a supernatural doctor. He saved Shawn's life from a fatal disease. It was a disease that plagued the elf race for centuries. Shawn, of course, pledged his life to this doctor. We thought he was a saint. For several years he healed elves all over the world. Everyone came to see the great doctor. The doctor was actually the one that developed several cures for diseases that tormented our people. Elves from far and wide pledged themselves to the doctor once he healed them from otherwise fatal sicknesses.

I don't know how Shawn found out, but we learned the doctor himself was responsible for many of the diseases in the first place. He was curing the diseases and gaining pledges to create his very own army of elves. He wanted to use us to take over the world.

Shawn came to me for help and we rallied some of the remaining elves that hadn't already pledged to him. There was a great battle and several of our friends and family lost their lives to the evil doctor. When it came down to the end, I should have been the one to finish the job. If I had been the one to kill the doctor, Shawn would have never turned dark. After that, it was too late. My brother was gone forever," Jack explained.

I noticed tears silently running down Jack's face. I looked around the room and saw that almost everybody had tears in their eyes.

"I am so sorry, Jack. I never knew," said Mom as she walked over and hugged Jack. She did what she could to comfort him.

"Can he be saved? Is there a way to reverse the dark curse?" Ava asked curiously.

"The council would never agree to it," said Jack sadly.

"Forget about the council, Jack. I know the dark one had done terrible things, but he isn't himself!" Shawn is an innocent man according to the story you just told," I said.

I suddenly remembered the horrible decision I had made by taking out all of the England vampires at Alexander's castle. I definitely didn't want to be responsible for something happening to another innocent man.

I heard vehicles pulling into headquarters from the elevator. I walked out of the hospital room in time to see Grandpa and his entourage of vehicles coming into headquarters.

"Something is up with the council," said Grandpa as he jumped from the vehicle. "They wouldn't even let us bring the dark one to them."

"What do you mean, Grandpa?" I asked.

"I called ahead to let them know we were bringing a prisoner. They told me they were not taking any more prisoners. Can you believe it? I'm beginning to wonder why we even have a council," Grandpa said raising his voice.

I could tell he was angry. I wondered what was really going on with the council.

"Well, I guess we will have to build our own prison!" I said. "If the council want take the bad guys we catch, where else can we put them? I asked.

"Why don't you just let me go?" said the dark elf as they unloaded him from the back of one of the SUVs.

"Take him to one of the holding cells downstairs until we can figure out what to do with him," I said. "I think we need to talk," I told Grandpa.

Grandpa's men took the dark one away while the rest of us headed into the conference room. I told Jack to tell Grandpa the story he told us about his brother. When he was finished, I waited for a reaction from Grandpa.

"So, the dark one is innocent? But, he must pay for the things he has done. He took my daughter!" Grandpa shouted.

"We're not saying he shouldn't pay for his crimes. What we are saying is that he is not himself. The elf behind the dark exterior is a great man. He saved the entire elf race by getting rid of that evil doctor," I explained.

"What should we do, Luke? He is your prisoner, so you should be the one to decide," said Grandpa.

That was definitely not the reaction I was expecting. I just knew Grandpa was going to have a fit about the suggestion we were making.

"I think we should try to reverse the dark curse and see what Shawn has to say," I said confidently.

"I agree. I guess you know how to do it?" Grandpa asked Ava.

"I'm sure I can figure it out!" Ava said excitedly.

I watched as Ava grabbed Jack's hand and led him out of the room with Cam hot on their heels. I knew they would come up with a solution in no time.

"So, what should we do about the situation with the council?" I asked once they were out of the room.

"The council has been worthless lately!" Grandpa exclaimed. "I think we should just forget about them. We should start construction of our own justice system."

"Really? You can't be serious," said Uncle Charles. "The council would never go for that."

"I don't care what the council will or won't go for! What kind of council refuses to take a criminal? What kind of council will not even help their people find loved ones? Certainly not any council I choose to be associated with!" Grandpa shouted.

I had never seen Grandpa so upset. I knew Grandpa meant what he saying. Nobody would be able to convince him otherwise because his decision had already been made. I agreed with everything he was saying. But, I didn't want to talk about another problem we had to fix.

"Can we talk about all of this stuff later? We just defeated our toughest enemy yet. I think we need a break," I said.

The next few days were busy as usual. Grandpa and I worked on finding a place for our new justice system. We conducted meetings with contractors and realtors about building an underground prison that could house the criminals I knew the soldiers would be apprehending. It was a work in progress to say the least. It would take months of hard work to establish what Grandpa and I were developing. It was quite amazing how well we worked together on a project as big and important as this one.

Ava and Jack had put together a spell to remove the dark curse. Once it was completed it worked great of course. Shawn was no longer plagued by the dark curse. He had no memory of the things he had done. We knew for sure after Jenna used her powers like she had with Adriana a few years back. When Shawn found out what happened he insisted that he pay for the crimes that he committed. Technically it wasn't him doing any of the horrible things. I don't think he will spend much time behind bars before we let him out to work his time off. I know we will find something productive for him to do. Jack spends most of his time outside his brother's cell. Cam is usually right there with them.

Mom and Dante were busy making plans to finish getting married. To our surprise, even with everything that had happened, Susan agreed to marry Uncle Charles. They actually planned to have a double wedding. Everyone was excited as the big day approached. Grandpa spared no expense in the preparations for both of his children to get married. Everyone could tell he was very proud of them.

When the wedding day finally rolled around, I couldn't help but be nervous. I kept waiting for the dark one to reappear at the altar. Ava tried her best to calm and comfort me, but I think she was just as nervous as I was. Luckily, the wedding went off without a hitch. It was amazing that my whole family was able to spend the whole day together doing something normal for a change. I hoped there were many more days to come just like it.

"Congratulations!" I said as I hugged Mom at the reception.

I even gave Dante a hug. I could tell he was very happy. I knew he was going to take great care of my mother.

"Congratulations!" Jenna said as she too gave them both hugs.

"We have something to tell both of you after the reception," said Mom. I couldn't imagine what it was. Surely it wasn't going to be bad news on such a joyous day.

The reception turned out great. Everyone laughed and danced and had an amazing time. Mom and Dante planned to leave for their honeymoon as soon as the reception was over. They didn't tell anybody where they were going. I had secretly packed their luggage into one of the two seated Travelports. Walter had built several more and I asked for a couple of them. I decorated it with shaving cream and streamers. I even tied cans to the back. I wanted them to be able to go anywhere in the world they chose as my wedding gift to them.

Jenna and I met Mom and Dante in the great room just as they were getting ready to leave.

"We wanted to tell you the good news before we leave," said Mom.

It was a huge relief to know it was going to be good news. But, what could she possibly be going to tell us? I asked myself.

"What is it Mom? You've had us waiting and wondering all day!" I said.

"You guys are going to be big brother and sister," Mom said excitedly.

"Really?" I asked.

"That's awesome!" shouted Jenna. "I always wanted a little brother or sister." Jenna rushed to give Mom a hug.

"Yeah that's great!" I said as I hugged Mom too.

I was excited by the thought of being a big brother. But, I was nervous about a new baby being brought into our very chaotic lives. I would never let Mom know I was anything other than happy about the new baby.

"Everyone is ready!" Ava said excitedly as she stuck her head in the door to the great room.

"So where are you guys going?" I asked.

"I'll send you a postcard, baby," Mom said smiling.

I couldn't believe she wouldn't even tell me. Why was it such a big secret about where they were going? I figured they didn't want to be bothered. I suddenly wished Ava and I could go somewhere and not be bothered.

"Oh, Luke, you shouldn't have!" Mom exclaimed as she came out the front door of the mansion. She spotted the Travelport sitting in the driveway.

There were actually two of them sitting there I noticed. Both decorated as though this were a normal human wedding. I looked over to Matt as he congratulated his dad and Susan. I saw him wink at me and a little grin formed at the corner of his mouth. It was his thank you for giving them use of the other Travelport.

"You guys can go anywhere and everywhere you choose. This will take you anywhere in the world in a matter of minutes," I said excitedly.

"Thank you, Luke," Dante said.

"You're welcome," I said giving him another hug.

I felt so comfortable around Dante. I had grown to like him a lot. I hoped one day I would have the chance to love him as a father. The thought brought a smile to my face.

"You guys get out of here and have fun!" Jenna said.

Mom and Dante walked hand in hand toward the Travelport. Everyone clapped and cheered as both couples climbed into the Travelport machines. The familiar voice asked them for their destination. I heard Uncle Charles say Hawaii. I guessed Susan played a big part in that decision. I didn't see my uncle as the beach lounging type.

I waited for Dante or my mom to say where they were going, but it never came as the windows slid closed. I guessed Dante had been slick and typed their destination into the screen. Very sneaky, I thought as a giggle escaped from my mouth.

"What's so funny?" Ava asked taking my hand in hers.

Just as the Travelports started to rise my vision went black and Nhados holding the infant came into focus. This time the vision didn't flash through the other images of the boys standing next to Nhados. I stared at him holding the helpless little boy. My heart sank into my stomach as the last piece of the puzzle went together. I now realized I knew somebody having a baby!

I woke up on my feet again as an uncontrollable growl escaped from deep within my body. I think I almost shifted into my wolf form during the vision. Luckily I was able to prevent that, but the growl escaped just the same.

"Luke, what's wrong?" Ava said as she held on to me.

I looked around and noticed several others in the crowd were staring at me. I attempted to calm myself but I was too worked up from the vision.

"Luke! Calm down and tell me what is going on," I heard Ava say.

"He is not getting my brother!" I growled, still on the verge of uncontrollably transforming into my wolf form.

Everyone looked to the sky as the two Travelports shot off in completely different directions. My life will never be normal, I thought as my body continued to tremble. The only thing helping me keep it together was Ava's loving embrace.

12243546R00152

Made in the USA
San Bernardino, CA
13 June 2014